Last Letters of Jacopo Ortis

Last Letters of Jacopo Ortis
and Of Tombs

Ugo Foscolo

Translated by J.G. Nichols

ET REMOTISSIMA PROPE

100 PAGES

100 PAGES

Published by Hesperus Press Limited

4 Rickett Street, London SW6 1RU

www.hesperuspress.com

Introduction and English language translation © J.G. Nichols, 2002

Of Tombs English language translation © J.G. Nichols, 1995, 2002

Foreword © Valerio Massimo Manfredi, 2002

Designed and typeset by Fraser Muggeridge

Printed in the United Arab Emirates by Oriental Press

ISBN: 1-84391-002-0

CONTENTS

For most passengers who travel on the London Underground from Heathrow to Victoria Station, Turnham Green is only one of a number of stops on the way. But for a classically educated Italian that name immediately evokes the powerful memory and the prophetic verse of one of our greatest poets. This was Ugo Foscolo, who died there, alone and completely forgotten, after harrowing torments, on 10th September 1827, at the age of forty-nine. That was in the early years of the Risorgimento, an insurrectionary movement which led to the liberation and reunification of the Italian nation after it had been divided and effectively lost to history for more than thirteen centuries. Foscolo had been desperately enthusiastic for this dream to be accomplished, and to it he had sacrificed his peace of mind and tranquil way of life, preferring a bold, adventurous course, shunning compromise and duplicity, guided by a proud, disdainful conscience.

He did not have the comfort of seeing the dawn break over his homeland, but when Italy was reunified, half a century later, his remains were brought to rest with those of Machiavelli, Alfieri, and Michelangelo in Florence's Church of Santa Croce, which he himself had celebrated in his poem *Of Tombs* as a shrine to Italy's great men. This fulfilled the wish he had expressed in one of his most moving sonnets:

> *O foreign peoples, send my bones at least*
> *Back to the breast of her who always mourns.*

The course taken by Foscolo's poetic evolution is unusual. He was born in Zante of a Greek mother and a Venetian father in 1778. He composed his first work at the age of only nineteen. This was the epistolary novel, entitled *Last Letters of Jacopo Ortis*, which is now being issued in this new English translation. Although inspired by other illustrious literary precedents, such as Goethe's *Sorrows of Young Werther*, it was above all the result of the first grievous disappointment in Foscolo's life. It was a political disappointment which nevertheless touched the deepest feelings of that young writer and poet who had been brought up on the classics and encouraged to venerate Greek and

Roman civilisation. It was Napoleon's cession of the Venetian Republic to Austria by the Treaty of Campoformio. To appreciate just how serious disappointment this was, we need to remember that Napoleon had at first been enthusiastically welcomed in Italy, indeed almost as a liberator. He was born an Italian (a year before the island of Corsica was ceded by the Genoese Republic to France) and for this reason it was thought that he must bring help to his country of origin. But Foscolo certainly never expected anything of the kind. Man of action that he was, he thought that there was only one way for people to regain their lost liberty – arms:

> 'They cry out that they have been sold and betrayed. But if they had taken up arms, they might have been conquered, yet not betrayed, and if they had defended themselves to the last drop of blood, the conquerors [i.e. Napoleon] could not have sold them, nor the conquered [i.e. the Austrians] dared to buy them.' (*Last Letters of Jacopo Ortis*)

And Foscolo was not scandalised by the cynical action of Napoleon when, in order to get himself accepted as one of the crowned heads of Europe, he did not hesitate to sell Venice to the Austrians:

> 'I do not complain of reasons of state which lead nations to be sold like flocks of sheep. So it always was, and so it always will be. I mourn for my homeland…' (*Last Letters of Jacopo Ortis*)

So Jacopo Ortis, the hero of the novel, while certainly an idealised character, has strong autobiographical elements, especially when he expresses his author's thoughts directly and explicitly. No form of narrative could have been more effective, for Foscolo's purpose, than the epistolary novel in which the protagonist Jacopo writes to his friend Lorenzo almost every day and sometimes more than once in the same day, composing a sort of diary of his unhappy love for Teresa and the loss of all hope for the future of his homeland. The narrative fiction makes very successful use of various expedients, such as passages that are incomplete, connecting sections, and comments by the editor, who is none other than Jacopo's friend to whom most of the letters are addressed. *Ortis* has been variously judged by the critics, and there are some who consider that the work has not achieved genuine literary merit, because it is not pure narration and yet does not reach poetical heights, and so can be regarded as a sort of hybrid, a first abortive attempt by the great poet of *Of Tombs* and the sonnets, which are his most noble and famous works. In reality *Ortis* already contains all those themes dear to Foscolo which were to be developed fully in the works that followed, in particular a dark pessimism concerning the human race ('man is an oppressive creature') and also concerning Nature who beguiles and deceives her children, making the dream of happiness through love flash into their minds solely to induce them to unite and procreate more unhappy creatures. Thus Jacopo, romantic hero and 'alter ego' of Ugo Foscolo, ardent patriot and impassioned lover, finds, at the age of only twenty-four, that he has drained the bitter cup of disillusion and deceit to the dregs, with his homeland sold and his beloved Teresa about to be joined to another man in an arranged marriage of interest. Nothing remains to give a meaning to Jacopo's life, and he prepares his suicide with extreme lucidity, as a conscious and thought-out decision, an act of rebellion against that blind cosmic mechanism which damns humankind to unhappiness and desperation.

To the modern reader *Ortis* may at first sight seem to be a difficult and inaccessible work, but we must remember both the time in which it was written and the kind of culture which produced it. In the first half of the nineteenth century ancient and almost forgotten pivotal nations like Greece and Italy, cradles of two great civilisations, the foundations of European culture, had finally roused themselves, and intellectuals of the time felt so very strongly the fascination and charm of this reawakening that some of them went off gladly to take part in those peoples' struggles for independence. We need think only of Lord Byron, or of the Italian Santorre di Santarosa who died at Sfacteria fighting against the Turks in 1821, or simply of Beethoven who wrote his Turkish March to celebrate the independence of Greece. It was a mystique of memory, a secular and libertarian mystique which perceived the identity of peoples and nations in their cultural inheritance, and in great and noble enterprises the only hope of immortality. This mystique, present already in *Ortis*, found its full development in the ode *Of Tombs*, a work of Foscolo's maturity:

> *The urns of strong men stimulate strong minds*
> *To deeds of great distinction...*

Ortis is, therefore, not quite achieved as a literary experience, but it does contribute to bringing into focus, so to speak, the figure of the Romantic hero who became the great fictional protagonist of the nineteenth century. It is, moreover, a formative novel because of its elevated and almost epic conception of love, and because of the political passion and civic commitment which characterise it, both of which are indispensable for the development of a modern society.

The gloomy sepulchral Romantic influence, typical of the works of Ossian and assimilated by Foscolo both in *Ortis* and in the sonnets and other poems which followed, is transformed in his poetry where it gains a sort of luminosity and even generates the hope of a wholly human immortality, granted not by a God who is unable to comfort men in their miseries, but by the solidarity which unites companions in misfortune and gives them everlasting gratitude for the memory of those who have sacrificed their own lives for others, who have not bowed down to tyranny, who have faced the bitterness of exile rather than submit to arbitrary power and injustice.

This dream of Foscolo's is a heroic one, populated by titanic shades – Dante, Alfieri, Galileo – and the ghosts of the ancient epics of Greece, his native land, which assume bodily form as they renew for ever the tremendous encounter between the oppressors and those who fight for liberty:

> *... The mariner*
> *Sailing that sea which lies beneath Euboea*
> *Observed beyond the spacious dark the lightning*
> *Of flashing helmets and of clashing swords,*
> *The pyres of blazing smoke, and saw the shapes*
> *Of spectral warriors in burnished arms*
> *Seek out the battle...*

This is the mystique of the good death (like that of Ortis who plunges a dagger into his heart as a final act of rebellion) which leaves behind it a noble memory and an inheritance of gratitude and affection.

Civic passion, therefore, depth of feeling, the spirit of liberty, but also compassion for the poor, contempt for the rich who believe that even human dignity may be bought, love for defenceless creatures – all these themes are to be found, in a disordered and at times hazy way, in the pages of *Ortis*, pages which are not yet settled and mature, but which to the eyes of modern men seem ingenuous or even disconcerting in that strident desperation which, while occasionally self-satisfied and narcissistic, is sincere and coherent. Foscolo's social sensitivity is unexpectedly apparent here and there in the pages of the novel and leaves one amazed by its almost anarchic lucidity:

> 'If there were no laws protecting those who, in order to enrich themselves with the sweat and tears of their fellow-citizens, drive them into need and crime, would gaols and executioners be so necessary?'

Unlike so many other artists, Foscolo played his part in life like a great actor. He was the ardent lover of beautiful women, proud of his military achievements and of his wounds sustained in battle, and inflexible with men of power who tried to flatter him and get him on their side. Carlo Cattaneo, another great Italian, a precursor of federalist political theories, said of him, 'He gave to Italy a new institution – exile.'

Even though he had judged Napoleon to be cynical, opportunistic, and sly, he did not in fact support the restoration which followed Napoleon's defeat. When the Austrian Government offered him a lavish salary as editor of a literary paper, at first he pretended to accept and then fled, to Lugano, to Zurich, and finally to England. He did what his hero, Jacopo Ortis, would have done if he had found himself in a similar situation. He was reckless, prodigal, and a squanderer of his own and other people's fortunes. He even dissipated the endowment of his daughter Floriana, building a grandiose villa which he called Digamma (in memory of his studies on a consonant of the Aeolic dialect) and burdened himself with debts which he could not repay. To stay out of prison, he had to hide his identity under the pseudonym of 'Mr Emerytt'. And yet not even in that wretched situation did he ever compromise his conscience as a free man. In the London fogs he dreamed of returning to his native island, Zante, knowing well that his dream was impossible:

> *I'll not set foot upon your sacred shore*
> *Ever, Zante, again! My earliest years*
> *Were cradled there, mirrored by waters where*
> *Out of the Grecian waves the goddess rose,*
> *Venus, our nurse...*

He died a peaceful twilit death in his daughter's arms. Death restored his stature. His work made him worthy to sleep under the majestic vaults of Santa Croce, close by Michelangelo, Galileo, and Alfieri whom he so greatly admired in life and to whom he had dedicated lines which now suited his own immutable condition:

> *With these great men for ever, he inspires*
> *Love of his native land.*

–Valerio Massimo Manfredi, 2002

There are memorials to Ugo Foscolo on the Ionian island of Zante, in Florence, and in London. Foscolo was born in Zante in 1778, when it was under Venetian control: in *Last Letters of Jacopo Ortis* he refers to the Ionian Islands more than once as 'the once Venetian islands', since by then they had passed into French hands. His father was Venetian, and his mother Greek. After his father's death, when Foscolo was still a very young child, the family settled in Venice, the 'homeland' mentioned so frequently in *Last Letters*. Foscolo fought under Napoleon, and was a member of the Italian division of the army which from 1804 to 1806 was poised in Northern France for an invasion of England which never took place. After Napoleon's final defeat at Waterloo in 1815 Foscolo came to England, where he lived in alternate extravagance and poverty. He died in 1827 in Turnham Green, at that time a village outside London, and was buried in Chiswick. In 1871, after the unification of Italy, his remains were removed and reinterred in Florence's Basilica of Santa Croce, among the other illustrious Italians whom he had celebrated in his poem *Of Tombs*. In 1939 the Fascist Government commissioned a statue of him to stand above his tomb: this shows him booted and spurred, a drum at his feet, and clutching his cloak around him defiantly with his left hand, while his right arm is in a sling.

Even such a brief account suggests some of the complications, paradoxes even, of Foscolo's life, and, since he was a very subjective writer, some of the complications of his art. He was only half Italian, and spent years fighting in an alien army; and yet he was an Italian patriot who longed for the unification and self-government of Italy which was achieved more than thirty years after his death. He was a lover of the Greek language, from which he made some translations, and an admirer of the classical balance and proportion which *Of Tombs* exemplifies; and yet *Last Letters* is, amongst other things, the portrayal of an unbalanced mind. Above all, he who loved liberty chose to serve in the armies of one of Europe's most notorious tyrants.

The complexities of Foscolo's life reflect not only his temperament but also the turbulent times in which he lived. The French Revolution, hailed by many in England and Europe as a blow struck for freedom, soon became a worse tyranny than that which it had replaced; and yet it kept, and even now for some still keeps, much of that glamour which it had for its champions at the time. (Perhaps that is because Napoleon did get rid of tyrants, even if it was only to replace them by his relatives.) So Foscolo remained in the service of the French even after, by the Treaty of Campoformio in 1797, Napoleon had ceded Venice to the Austrians, betraying the Italians who had trusted and helped him, and France had taken over the Ionian Islands, a particularly bitter pill for Foscolo to swallow.

Last Letters is most obviously a revelation of the intimate thoughts, ravings often, of an individual who bears a strong resemblance to Foscolo himself: Jacopo Ortis is disturbed by what has happened to his homeland, and also by his love for Teresa, a love which is returned but unfulfilled. These are personal themes, and they could hardly be presented in a more personal way than by private letters to a very close friend. Yet these personal matters are the subjective tip of an objective iceberg. That Jacopo's love of the unhappy Teresa has to be unfulfilled is the result of the social and political conditions of the time: Teresa's father must marry her to someone (the long-suffering Odoardo, treated in his letters with little respect by the self-obsessed Jacopo) who can help him mend his family's fortunes and also keep the T*** family safe from persecution. Then there is another layer of meaning: the crimes and misfortunes of the time are shown to be contemporary instances of what has occurred throughout human history: the good are always overcome by the bad; even the good are in many ways bad; and the individual is bound to suffer since 'every individual is a born enemy of society, because society is of necessity hostile to individuals.'

This view of history and of human institutions was, of course, much in the air at the time: one need only think of Rousseau. And it is not a view found only in that period. So Jacopo's wild outcries – in many ways those of a typical Romantic hero: self-centred, passionate, unrestrained, and finally suicidal – do reveal, not arguments so much as attitudes which have to be treated seriously. At times Jacopo seems scarcely sane, but one must beware of dismissing his thoughts as therefore unworthy of consideration. One remark by Jacopo, which tempts the reader to dismiss it as the exaggeration of a wandering mind, may be cited as an extreme example of a method typical of the book as a whole. In the last letter of Part One Jacopo out of the blue says, 'But I too am a killer.' Oh yes, a figurative killer, one thinks. But, as is made clear only much later, the killing is all too literal.

Some of the *Last Letters* contain ideas which are developed in *Of Tombs*. For instance the letter headed 27th August in Part Two begins: 'Just now I have been adoring the tombs of Galileo, Machiavelli, and Michelangelo…' The novel and the poem have much in common: like *Last Letters* the poem is rhapsodic, and its transitions are by no means always obvious.

The poem also has precedents and in many ways fits readily into the tradition of graveyard poems, a tradition best represented in England by Gray's *Elegy*, which is quoted as an epigraph to the *Last Letters* and echoed in other parts of that work. It is interesting that in Italy Foscolo's poem has the same widespread acclaim as Gray's has in England.

Two features distinguish Foscolo's poem. One is its central theme, which is not a common one: to the materialist, such as Foscolo gives himself out to be, tombs can do nothing for the dead; but they can inspire the living to virtuous and noble action in imitation of the dead. Foscolo goes out of his way to stress this contrast: the agnosticism of *Last Letters* becomes in the poem atheism, and all hope of life beyond the tomb is explicitly denied; so the inspirational effect of appropriate tombs seems all the more important.

The other distinguishing mark of the poem is its style. Despite the rapidity of the thoughts, it is always balanced and controlled. A mixture of lament for human mortality and praise for the honourable dead, with passages of an epic nature, it maintains its impetus and its high tone throughout. Contemporary allusions are mixed with classical ones; but all are seen in the same timeless light of myth, and so they represent the condition of mortals throughout the ages.

– *J.G. Nichols*, 2002

ACKNOWLEDGEMENTS

This translation of *Ultime lettere di Jacopo Ortis* is made from the edition by Enzo Bottasso: *Poesie e prose d'arte di Ugo Foscolo* (UTET, Turin, third edition, 1968) which follows the last version prepared by Foscolo for the press (1817).

The translation of *Dei sepolcri* (also made from the edition above) has already been published in *Translation and Literature*, Volume 4, Part 1 (1995).

I wish to thank Alessandro Gallenzi for clarifying some points in the Italian which were to me obscure; and also Joseph Griffiths for identifying the source of the quotation from Lucan on p. 126 below.

Last Letters
of Jacopo Ortis

Naturae clamat ab ipso vox tumulo.[1]

TO THE READER

My intention in publishing these letters is to raise a monument to unknown virtue, and to consecrate to the memory of my only friend those tears which now I am forbidden to shed upon his tomb. And you, gentle reader, if you are not one of those who demand from others that heroism of which they are themselves incapable, will, I hope, extend your compassion to this unhappy youth from whom you may perhaps take comfort and example.

– Lorenzo Alderani

Part One

The sacrifice of our homeland is complete. All is lost, and life remains to us – if indeed we are allowed to live – only so that we may lament our misfortunes, and our shame. My name is on the list of those proscribed, I know, but would you wish me to save myself from my oppressor by giving myself over to him who has betrayed me? Comfort my mother: overcome by her tears I have obeyed her, and I have left Venice in order to escape the first, and most ferocious, persecutions. And must I now forsake even this long-accustomed solitude of mine, where, without losing sight of my unhappy land, I may still hope for some days of peace? You make me shudder, Lorenzo. Just how many unfortunates are there? And even we Italians, alas, are washing our hands in Italian blood. I do not mind what happens to me: since I despair both of my homeland and of myself, I am waiting placidly for imprisonment and death. At least my dead body will not fall into the hands of strangers. My name will be quietly mourned by a few good men, the companions of our miseries, and my bones will rest in our ancestral earth.

13TH OCTOBER

I beg you, Lorenzo, to insist no more. I am determined not to leave these hills. It is true that I promised my mother I would take refuge in some other country, but I haven't the heart to do it, and she will forgive me, I hope. Is this life worth preserving by cowardice and exile? Oh how many of our fellow-citizens will moan and groan and repent, far from their homes, the fact that they have done that! And what could we ourselves expect but penury and scorn? Or at best some brief and fruitless compassion, the sole comfort which civilised nations afford to the alien refugee. And where should I look for shelter? In Italy, that prostituted country, always the victor's reward? Could I have before my eyes those who have despoiled, derided, and sold us, and not weep for anger? To the ruin of whole peoples, they exploit what they call liberty as the popes exploited crusades. Ah, how often in despair of vengeance I feel like plunging a knife into my heart to pour out all my blood amid the last shrieks of my homeland!

And these others? They have bought our slavery, regaining with gold what they stupidly and cravenly lost in war. Truly I am like one of those wretches who, having been given out for dead, were buried alive, and then, coming round, found themselves in the tomb among shadows and skeletons, certain that they were living, but in despair of the pleasant light of day, and forced to die amid curses and hunger. Why let us see and experience liberty, and then take it back for ever, and so shamefully?

Enough of that, let us speak no more of it. The storm seems to have died down. If the danger returns, be assured, I shall try every means of escape. However, I am living peacefully, as peacefully as anyone can. I see no one at all, I am always wandering through the countryside. But, to tell you the truth, I think, and I am troubled. Send me some books.

How is Lauretta? Poor girl! When I left her she was beside herself. She is beautiful and still young, but her mind is unstable, and she is so sad at heart. I did not love her, but out of either pity or gratitude, if she had chosen me alone to comfort her, pouring into my ear all her soul and her weaknesses and her sufferings – I would indeed gladly have made her my lifelong companion. Fate did not wish it. Better so, perhaps. She loved Eugenio, and he died in her arms. Her father and her brothers have had to flee from their homeland, and that poor family, deprived of all human help, is left to live, who can tell how, on tears. There, O Liberty, is another victim for you. Do you know that as I write to you, Lorenzo, I am weeping like a child? It is only too true! I have always become involved with bad people, and if occasionally I have met someone good, I have always had to feel sorry for him. Farewell, farewell.

Michele has brought me the Plutarch, for which I thank you. He told me you would send some more books on another occasion. I have enough for now. The divine Plutarch will console me for the crimes and miseries of humanity as I turn my eyes on the few illustrious men who, more or less pre-eminent among mankind, stand out from so many centuries and so many peoples. I do fear however that, if they were stripped of their historical splendour and of our reverence for antiquity, there would not be much to boast about concerning the ancients, or the moderns, or myself. Ah, the human race!

If I can ever hope for peace, it is here, Lorenzo. The parish priest, the doctor, and all the obscure beings in this part of the world have known me since I was a child and are fond of me. Although I am living here as a fugitive, they all gather round me as though they wanted to tame a noble wild beast. For the moment I just let them get on with it. Admittedly I have not had such good treatment from human beings as to lead me to trust them straightaway. But on the other hand, the tyrant's way of life, in fear and trembling of having his throat cut any minute, seems to me like the agony of a slow death, a shameful thing. At noon I sit with them under the plane tree by the church reading the lives of Lycurgus and Timoleon to them. On Sunday all the peasants crowded round me. Although they understood nothing at all, they listened to me open-mouthed. I believe that the wish to know and retell the history of past times stems from our self-love which would like to be deceived and prolong our life by uniting it with people and things that are no more, making them, so to speak, our own property. The imagination loves to roam through the centuries and possess another universe. With what emotion an old workman this morning told me about the lives of the priests of this parish in his childhood, and described to me the damage done by the storm of thirty-seven years ago, and the times of plenty, and the times of hunger. He wandered from the point every now and then, but always came back to it, and excused himself for his lapses! In this way I manage to forget that I am alive.

I have had a visit from Signor T*** whom you met in Padua. He told me that you often spoke to him about me, and that the day before yesterday you wrote to him about me. He too has taken refuge in the country to escape the initial fury of the mob, although to tell the truth he has not been much involved in public affairs. I had heard that he was an educated man of the highest probity – qualities which used to be respected, but cannot now be possessed with impunity. He is courteous, has an open countenance, and speaks from the heart.

There was someone with him, his daughter's fiancé I think. No doubt he is a fine young man, but his face tells me nothing. Good night.

I have at last caught by the scruff of the neck that rogue of a peasant-boy who was destroying our kitchen garden, cutting and breaking everything that he could not steal. He was up a peach tree, while I was in a pergola. He was happily breaking off the branches that were still green, because there was no more fruit on them. As soon as I had him in my clutches, he began to cry out for mercy. He confessed to me that for weeks he had been engaged in that wicked business because the gardener's brother had some months previously stolen a sack of broad beans from his father. 'And your father teaches you to steal?' 'Truly, sir, everyone does it.' I let him go, and jumping over a hedge I cried out, 'That is society in miniature: they are all like that.'

26TH OCTOBER

I have seen her, Lorenzo, 'the divine maiden', and I thank you for it. I found her seated, painting a miniature of herself. She rose to her feet, greeting me as though she knew me, and told a servant to go and look for her father. 'He did not dare to hope you would come,' she told me. 'He is probably in the fields. It won't be long before he returns.' A little girl was running round her knees, saying I don't know what in her ear. Teresa said to her, 'This is a friend of Lorenzo. It was he whom Daddy went to see the day before yesterday.' In the meantime Signor T*** had returned. He greeted me with familiarity, thanking me for remembering him. Teresa meanwhile, taking her little sister by the hand, went away. 'Look,' he said to me, pointing to his daughters as they were leaving the room, 'that is all there is of us.' He ventured these words, it seemed to me, as if he wanted to let me know that his wife was not there. He did not mention her. We chatted for a good while. When I was about to leave, Teresa came back. 'We are not so very far away,' she said to me. 'Come and spend some evenings with us.'

I went home with my heart full of joy. What can I say? Is the sight of beauty enough to lay to rest all the sufferings of us sad mortals? You see there is a well-spring of life in me. Certainly the only one, and, who knows, perhaps a fatal one. But if my soul is predestined to be perpetually in a storm, does it matter?

28TH OCTOBER

Please be silent, please be silent. There are days when I cannot trust myself: a demon burns me, shakes me, consumes me. Perhaps I have a high opinion of myself, but it seems to me impossible that our homeland should be so oppressed while we are still living. What are we doing all this time living among regrets? In short, I beg you not to speak to me about it any more. When you tell me of our sufferings, which are so many, are you perhaps reproaching me for staying here in indolence? And do you not realise that you are torturing me with a thousand martyrdoms? Oh, if there were only one tyrant, and the slaves were less stupid, my right hand would suffice. But he who blames me now for cowardice, would accuse me then of a crime. And the wise man himself would pity in me, not the prudence of the strong man, but the frenzy of the madman. What action would you suggest taking, caught between two powerful nations which – inveterate, sworn, ferocious enemies of each other – unite only in order to throw us into chains? And where their strength is not enough, one deceives us with enthusiasm for liberty, the other with religious fanaticism. And all of us, cowardly slaves ruined by ancient servitude and recent licentiousness, moan and groan, betrayed and starving and never provoked either by betrayal or starvation. Ah, if I could, I would bury my home, my dearest friends, and myself, in order to leave nothing, nothing to make those nations proud of their omnipotence and my servitude! There were races once who, rather than obey the Romans, the world's brigands, gave to the flames their homes, their wives, their children, and themselves, burying their sacred independence among the glorious ruins and ashes of their homeland.

1ST NOVEMBER

I am well. I am well for the time being, like an invalid who is asleep and does not feel his pain, and whole days pass by in the house of Signor T*** who loves me like a dear son. I let myself be beguiled, and the apparent happiness of that family seems to me to be real, and

11

to be mine also. If only that fiancé did not exist! Because in fact…
I hate no one in the world, but there are certain men whom I want
only to see from a distance. His future father-in-law came to me
yesterday evening singing his praises as though he were writing a
letter of commendation: *good… correct… patient!* And was there
nothing else he could say? Even if he possessed those virtues to a
degree of angelic perfection, with that heart which is always so dead,
and that masterful face never animated either by a smile of pleasure or
by the gentle silence of compassion, he would be for me like one of
those rose bushes with no flowers which make me fear the thorns.
What is a man if he is given over to cold, calculating reason? Wicked,
and wicked in a contemptible way. On the other hand Odoardo
knows something of music, he plays a good game of chess, he eats, he
reads, he sleeps, he walks – and all as if by clockwork. And he never
speaks emphatically, except to extol, as he does continually, his
sumptuous, select library. But when he goes on repeating, in that
pedantic voice of his, 'sumptuous and select' I feel ready to give him
the lie outright. If all the ravings of mankind which under the name of
science or *learning* have been written down and printed in every age
and by every race, were reduced to a thousand volumes at most, it
seems to me that we presumptuous mortals would have no reason to
complain. Let's have an end of all these discourses.

Meanwhile I have started to educate Teresa's little sister. I am
teaching her to read and to write. When I am with her, my face
brightens up, my heart is more joyful than it has ever been, and I play a
thousand boyish pranks. I don't know why, but children always like
me. And that little girl really is sweet! With her curly blond hair, her
blue eyes, her rosy cheeks, fresh, innocent, and chubby, she looks, for
all her four years, like one of the Three Graces. If you saw her run to
me, grasp my knees, run away to make me follow her, deny me a kiss
and then suddenly put those little lips to mine! Today I was at the top
of a tree gathering fruit: that dear creature held out her arms and
stammered, 'Please don't fall.'

What a beautiful autumn! Goodbye, Plutarch! He stays under my
arm, unopened. For three days I spent the morning filling a basket
with grapes and peaches which I covered with leaves. I followed the

course of the brook, and when I got to the house, I roused the whole household by singing the harvest song.

12TH NOVEMBER

Yesterday, which was a holiday, we ceremonially transplanted the pines from the nearby hillock to the hill opposite the church. My father likewise tried to make that small hill fertile, but the cypresses which he put there have never managed to flourish, and the pines are still young. Helped by a few workmen I crowned the summit, down which the water tumbles, with five poplars, shading the eastern side with a dense grove which will be the first thing to be greeted by the sun when he appears in his splendour at the crest of the mountains. And in fact yesterday the sun, more bright than usual, warmed the air up again, chilled as it was by the mist of the dying autumn. At noon the peasant-girls came in their holiday-smocks, enlivening the games and dances with their songs and toasts. One was the bride, one the little daughter, and another the sweetheart of one of the workmen. And you know that our peasants have a custom, when trees are transplanted, of converting their hard work into pleasure, since they believe, in the ancient tradition of their grandfathers and great-grandfathers, that without some ceremonial glasses of wine, the trees could not take firm root in the strange earth.

Meanwhile I was imagining a winter's day like this in the distant future when, my hair now white, I shall move very slowly along on my stick, taking comfort in the rays of the sun which are so precious to the old, greeting, as they come out of church, the bent country-people who were once my companions in the days when our limbs were strong with youth, and delighting in the fruits produced, however tardily, by the trees my father planted. In a feeble voice I shall recount our humble histories then to my, and your, little grandchildren, or to Teresa's: they will be frisking around me. And when my cold bones are sleeping beneath that little grove, which by then will be luxuriant and shady, perhaps on summer evenings the melancholy murmur of the leaves will be united with the sighs of the old fathers of the villa, who at the sound of the passing-bell will pray for the repose of the soul of 'that good old man', and will commend his memory to their children. And when at times the weary reaper comes there for some relief from the heat of June, he will cry out when he sees my grave, 'He it was who created this fresh hospitable shade!' O illusions! How can he who has no homeland say, 'I shall leave my ashes here, or leave them there'?

> *People were happy! Everyone knew once*
> *Where he'd be buried, and there was as yet*
> *No bed deserted for the sake of France.*[2]

20TH NOVEMBER

Several times I have started to write this letter, but the thing has dragged on and on, and the beautiful day, my promise to be at the villa early, and the solitude... You are laughing? The day before yesterday and yesterday itself I awakened with the intention of writing to you, and then without realising it I found myself out of doors.

It's raining, it's hailing, it's thundering and lightening. I think I shall make a virtue of necessity and take advantage of this hellish day to write to you. Six or seven days ago we went on a pilgrimage. Nature was looking more beautiful than ever. Teresa, her father, Odoardo, the little Isabella, and I went on a visit to Petrarch's house in Arquà. Arquà is, as you know, four miles from my home, but to shorten the way we took the steep road. A most beautiful autumn day was just breaking. Night, followed by the shadows and the stars, seemed to be in flight before the sun which was issuing in great splendour from the eastern clouds, like the lord of the universe, and the universe was smiling. The clouds, gilded and tinged with a thousand colours, were climbing up the clear vault of heaven which looked almost as if it were revealing itself for the purpose of shedding upon mortal beings the Godhead's loving care. At every step I greeted the family of flowers and plants as they gradually raised their heads which were bent beneath the hoar frost. The trees, gently rustling, made the transparent drops of dew flicker against the light, while the dawn winds were washing the superfluous liquid from the plants. You might have heard a solemn harmony spreading confusedly throughout the woods, the birds, the flocks, the rivers, and the labours of mankind, and meanwhile the breathing air was perfumed with the exhalations which the exulting earth sent up from the valleys and hills to the sun, Nature's chief minister. I pity that wretch who can awake in silence and coldly regard such blessings without feeling his eyes bathed in tears of thankfulness. Then it was I saw Teresa in all the glorious trappings of her grace. Although she gave a general impression of gentle melancholy, she was animated by a frank, lively joyfulness which came straight from the heart. Her voice was muted, her large dark eyes, at first wide open in delight, started to go moist. All her strength seemed to be invaded by the sacred beauty of the countryside. In such fullness of emotion souls open themselves up to pour their feelings into another's breast: and she turned to Odoardo. O God in heaven! he was like one groping in the shades of night or in deserts where Nature's blessings are unknown. All of a sudden she turned from him, and leant on my arm, saying to me... But, Lorenzo, however much I try to go on, it is better that I fall silent. Could I only convey to you her utterance, her gestures, the melody of her voice, her heavenly countenance, or if nothing else, reproduce her words without altering or shifting one syllable of them, I know you would be grateful to me: but, knowing that I can't, I would be annoyed with myself. What is the use of making an imperfect copy of an inimitable picture, when its fame alone gives a better idea of it than the wretched copy does? And does it not seem to you that I am like those poets who translate Homer? Because you see me tiring myself out only in order to water down the feeling which inflames me and dissolve it in my feeble phraseology.

Lorenzo, I am tired of this. I shall finish my account tomorrow. The wind is roaring, but I want to try to make the journey. I shall remember you to Teresa.

Oh, heavens! I shall have to go on with my letter. Just outside my door there is a quagmire in the way. I could clear it in one bound – and then what? The rain does not stop. It is past midday, and there are only a few hours to go before night falls like the end of the world. Today is a day lost, Teresa.

'I am not happy,' Teresa said to me, and with those words she wrung my heart. I was walking by her side in a deep silence. Odoardo joined Teresa's father, and they went on in front of us, chatting. Isabella came behind us in the arms of the gardener. *I am not happy!* I realised all the terrible meaning of those words, and I groaned in my soul, having before my eyes the victim who had to be sacrificed to prejudice and interest. Teresa, noticing my silence, altered her tone and tried to smile. 'Some dear memories,' she said, but suddenly she dropped her eyes. I did not dare to reply.

We were already near Arquà, and as we descended the grassy slope, the hamlets, which a short while ago we could see scattered across the valleys beneath, faded from our sight. At last we found ourselves in an avenue bordered on one side by quivering poplars which let fall on our heads their more yellowish leaves, and shaded on the other side by lofty oaks, which in their silence and darkness contrasted with the pleasant green of the poplars. Every now and then the two lines of opposing trees were connected by odd branches of wild vine, which made so many curving festoons gently shaken by the morning wind. Teresa then stopped and looked around. 'Oh how often,' she broke out, 'have I stretched out on this grass under the cooling shade of these oaks! I came here many times last summer with my mother.' She fell silent and turned back, saying that she wanted to wait for Isabella who had fallen a little behind us. But I suspected that she had gone from me in order to hide the tears which flooded her eyes, and which perhaps she was not able to hold back any longer. 'But, but why,' I said to her, 'whyever is your mother not here?' 'For some weeks she has been living in Padua with her sister. She lives apart from us, and will do so perhaps for ever! My father loved her, but since he decided to give me a husband whom I cannot love, there has been no more peace in our family. My poor mother, after having vainly opposed this marriage, has gone away so that she might have no part in my inevitable unhappiness. Meanwhile I am forsaken by everyone! I have promised my father, and I do not wish to disobey him – but it grieves me all the more that it is through me that our family is so disunited – through me… but never mind!' And at these words, tears fell from her eyes. 'Please excuse me,' she added, 'I needed to give vent to the anguish in my heart. I can neither write to my mother nor receive any letters from her. My father, proud and resolute once he has made up his mind, does not wish to hear her mentioned. He is continually repeating to me that she is his and my worst enemy. Yet I feel that I do not love, I never shall love this fiancé with whom it is already *decreed*…' Imagine, Lorenzo, my situation at that moment. I could not comfort her, nor reply to her, nor counsel her. 'Please, please,' she resumed, 'don't distress yourself, I implore you. I have put my trust in you – the need to find someone able to sympathise with me – some fellow-feeling – I have no one but you.' O what an angel! Yes, yes! Could I weep for ever, and so wash away your tears! This wretched life of mine is yours, all yours. I dedicate it to you, and I dedicate it to your happiness!

How much unhappiness, Lorenzo, in one family! You can see what obstinacy there is in Signor T***, who is otherwise a fine honest gentleman. He loves his daughter deeply, he often praises her and looks at her with pride, and yet he holds a sword over her. Some days later Teresa told me how he, endowed with an ardent soul, has always lived consumed with unhappiness. His finances are in difficulties because of his munificence, and he is persecuted by those men who, in times of revolution, find their own fortunes on the ruin of others. Fearing for his children, he believes he can provide for his family by arranging a marriage with a man of sense, rich, and in expectation of a considerable inheritance – perhaps, Lorenzo, also because of his clouded way of thinking. And I would wager a hundred to one that he would not give his dear daughter in marriage to a man without the least nobility: *he who is born a patrician, dies a patrician.* To make it worse, he considers his wife's opposition a violation of his own authority, and this tyrannical leaning makes him even more inflexible. Nevertheless, he has a good heart, and that air of sincerity which he has, and that continual petting of his dear daughter, and at times quietly sympathising with her, show perhaps that he sees and laments the poor girl's sorrowful resignation. And this is why, when I see how men are fated inexorably to go looking for disasters, and how they lie awake, sweat, and weep in order to procure for themselves the most painful and enduring ones, I would blow my brains out rather than let such a temptation cross my mind.

I am leaving you now, Lorenzo. Michele is calling me to dinner. I shall come back to this letter in a little while, if I cannot do anything else.

The bad weather has cleared up, and this evening is very beautiful. The Sun is at last breaking through the clouds, and he is comforting Nature in her sadness, shedding his rays upon her face. I write facing the balcony, from which I gaze at the everlasting light which is gradually fading on the distant horizon radiant with fire. The air is calm once more, and the countryside, although flooded, and only embellished with trees that have already lost their leaves and strewn with plants that have been blown down, looks more cheerful than it did before the storm. Just so, Lorenzo, the man who is unhappy shakes off his bitter cares when there is a single gleam of hope, and beguiles his bad luck with pleasures to which he was utterly insensible when he lay lapped in blind prosperity. Meanwhile the day is going: I can hear the vespers. So here I am, about to finish off my account at last. We continued on our brief pilgrimage until we saw, white in the distance, the little house which at one time welcomed:

> *That Man whose fame the world cannot contain…*
> *Whose Laura had on earth celestial honours.*[3]

I approached the house like one about to prostrate himself on the tombs of his ancestors, or like one of those priests who used to frequent, in silent reverence, the woods inhabited by the gods. Owing to the impiety of the owners of this treasure, the sacred home of that sublime Italian is falling down. In vain will travellers come from distant lands and look with pious wonder for the room still echoing with the heavenly poems of Petrarch. Instead they will weep over a heap of ruins covered with nettles and weeds, in which the solitary fox perhaps has made its lair. O Italy, appease the shades of your great men! Oh, I groan to myself when I recall the last words of Torquato Tasso. He had lived forty-seven years amidst the derision of courtiers, the tedium of pedants, and the pride of princes, sometimes imprisoned and sometimes a vagrant, and always melancholy, sick, and poor. Then finally he lay on his deathbed and wrote, as he breathed his last sigh: *I have no wish to complain of fortune's malignity, not to mention the ingratitude of men who have longed for the triumph of bringing me to a pauper's grave.* O Lorenzo, these words are always resounding in my heart, and I think I know someone who will die one day repeating them!

Meanwhile, with my soul full of love and harmony, I recited under my breath the *canzone*: *Clear, fresh, and pleasant water*; and that other one: *From thought to thought, along each mountain-top*, and the sonnet: *Let us pause, Love, to see her and her worth*,[4] and as many others of those superhuman verses as my troubled memory could at that time bring to mind.

Teresa and her father had gone off with Odoardo who wished to look over the accounts of the steward of an estate which he has in that area. I learned afterwards that he was ready to leave for Rome, because a cousin of his had died. Apparently, he will not be able to return for quite some time, because the other relatives have taken possession of the property of the dead man, and the affair will have to go to court.

As soon as my friends returned, that family of farmers found us something to eat, after which we set off for home. Farewell, farewell. There are other things I might mention to you, but to tell you the truth, I am writing a bit carelessly. By the way, I forgot to tell you that, on the way home, Odoardo walked very slowly with Teresa, and spoke to her at length as if pestering her, and with a look of authority on his face. From the few words that I overheard, I suspect that he was tormenting her, to find out at any cost what we had spoken about. From which you can see that I must make my visits less frequent – at least until he goes away.

Good night, Lorenzo. Keep this letter. When Odoardo takes my happiness away with him, and I see Teresa no more, and when her innocent little sister no longer frolics on my knees, in those days of boredom when even grief is dear to us, we shall reread these memories stretched out on that slope which overlooks the solitude of Arquà, at the hour when daylight is fading. Recalling that Teresa was our friend will staunch our tears. Let us treasure those dear and tender feelings which may reawaken in us, through all the years – years of sadness and persecution perhaps – which lie before us, the memory that we have not always lived in sorrow.

22ND NOVEMBER

In three days, at the most, Odoardo will no longer be here. Teresa's father is to accompany him as far as the border. He gave me to understand that he would like me to make this short journey with him, but I thanked him and refused, because I am determined to go away. I shall go to Padua. I must not abuse the friendship and trust of Signor T***. 'Let my daughters enjoy your company,' he said to me this morning. Apparently, he thinks I am a veritable Socrates. *Me*? And with that angelic creature born to love and be loved? And so unhappy at the same time! And I am always so completely at one with those who are unhappy, because – truly – I find there is something wicked in a man who is thriving.

I don't know how he fails to notice that, when I speak of his daughter, I become confused and stammer. I change countenance and I stand like a thief before a judge. At that point I get lost in thought, and I want to curse heaven when I see in this man so many excellent gifts, all spoilt by his prejudices and his blind obduracy which will bring him bitter grief. This is how I consume my days, lamenting my own misfortunes and those of others.

And yet I am sorry I do that. I often laugh at myself, because in fact my heart cannot endure a moment, one single moment, of calm. Provided I am always agitated, it does not matter to my heart whether the winds are adverse or favourable. When pleasure is lacking, my heart immediately resorts to grief. Yesterday Odoardo came to me to return a shotgun which I had lent him, and to say his goodbyes. I could not see him go without throwing my arms round his neck, although really I ought to have copied his own indifference. O you people who are wise, I have no idea what name you give to someone who is only too ready to obey his own heart. Because he is certainly not a hero. But is he therefore a base coward? Those who treat passionate men like weak creatures resemble the doctor who called a sick man mad for no other reason than that he was overcome by a fever. So I hear rich men charge poor people with guilt simply because they are not rich. To me it all seems a matter of appearance, with no reality whatsoever. Men who cannot by themselves obtain their own and others' esteem endeavour to exalt themselves by comparing those defects which they happen not to have with those which their neighbour does have. But does the man who fails to get drunk because he has a natural aversion from wine, deserve praise for his sobriety?

O you who dispute so peacefully over the passions, if your cold hands did not find that everything they touched was cold, if whatever entered your icy heart did not immediately freeze, do you think you would be so proud of your stern philosophy? How can you discuss things with which you have no acquaintance?

So far as I am concerned, wise men may vaunt their sterile apathy. I read some time ago, in I know not what poet, that their virtue is a block of ice which attracts everything to itself and chills whoever draws near. *Neither does the Lord abide always in tranquil majesty; but he wraps himself up in the north winds, and with the tempests he walks.*[5]

27TH NOVEMBER

Odoardo has gone, and I shall go when Teresa's father returns. Goodbye.

3RD DECEMBER

This morning I went to the villa rather early, and I was already close to the T*** residence when I was brought to a standstill by the distant tinkling of a harp. My soul rejoiced within me as I felt so much pleasure flow through me from that sound! It was Teresa. How can I conjure you up, O heavenly creature, and call you to mind in all your beauty, without despair in my heart? Sad to say, you are starting to take your first sips from life's bitter chalice, and I shall see you unhappy with my own eyes, and I shall not be able to comfort you except by weeping! And I must be the one to advise you out of pity to be reconciled to your misfortune.

Certainly I could neither affirm nor deny to myself that I love her. But if I do love her, if I do – truly it is only with a love that, God knows, is unthinking!

I stopped dead on the spot, without even blinking, with my eyes, my ears, and all my senses alert, letting myself be treated like a god, in that place where there was no one in sight to make me blush for my ecstasy. Now put yourself in my shoes when I heard Teresa sing those stanzas of Sappho, those which I had translated as best I could together with the other two odes, all that remains of the poetry of that loving woman, immortal as the Muses themselves. With a start I went on, and I found Teresa in her boudoir on that very chair where I saw her the first day, when she was painting her own portrait. She was casually dressed in white, the treasure of her blond hair overspread her shoulders and breast, her divine eyes were bathed in pleasure, her whole face evinced a gentle languor, her rosy arm, her foot, her fingers softly playing the harp – all was in complete harmony, and I felt an unwonted delight in contemplating her. Although Teresa seemed confused, suddenly finding a man gazing at her, carelessly dressed as she was, and I was beginning to reproach myself silently for my importunity and boorishness, she nevertheless went on playing, and I dismissed all other desires except that of adoring her and listening to her. I cannot describe to you, my dear friend, the state in which I found myself. I do know that I no longer felt the weight of this mortal life.

With a smile she arose and left me alone. Little by little I came to myself again. I rested my head on that harp and my face was bathed in tears. Oh! My heart was a little lighter.

PADUA, 7TH DECEMBER

I hardly like to say it, but I very much fear that you have taken me at my word and moved heaven and earth to drive me from my pleasant hermitage. Yesterday Michele turned up to announce on my mother's behalf that my accommodation in Padua was ready. (I had said on a previous occasion – which in fact I can scarcely recall – that I wanted to withdraw there when the university reopened.) It is true that I had sworn to come here, and I wrote to you about it, but I was waiting for Signor T***, who has not yet returned. However, I have had the sense to realise where my true vocation lies, and I have abandoned my hills without saying goodbye to a living soul. Otherwise, despite your sermons and my good intentions, I would never have gone from there. And I confess to you that there is a certain bitterness in my heart, and that I often feel the temptation to go back. Well, now you know that I am in Padua and that I will soon become something of a wiseacre, so that you may stop lecturing me *that I am wasting myself in crazy things*. However, I shall not let you oppose me when I wish to go away. You do know I was born quite incapable in some ways, particularly of living the sort of life which study demands, at the expense of my peace of mind and my spirit's freedom – or rather, I will grant you this – of my whims.

Meanwhile, thank my mother, and to lessen her displeasure, predict, as though the idea came from yourself, that I shall not stay here for more than a month, or not much more.

PADUA, 11TH DECEMBER

I have made the acquaintance of the wife of the nobleman M***. She forsakes the turmoil of Venice and the home of her lazy husband to enjoy a large part of the year in Padua. What a pity! Her youthful beauty has already lost that modest naivety which alone radiates grace and love. Very skilled in feminine courtesies, she endeavours to please only in order to conquer, so at least it seems to me. However, who knows? She likes to be with me, and often murmurs to me in an undertone, and smiles when I praise her. Moreover she does not delight, as other women do, in that badinage known as bons mots and shafts of wit, always an indication of a mind that is naturally malicious. I must tell you that yesterday evening, moving her chair close to mine, she spoke of some of my verses, and as we went on to chat about such trifles, I mentioned a certain book which she then requested from me. I promised to take it to her this morning. It is nearly time. Goodbye.

TWO O'CLOCK

The servant pointed to a boudoir. I had scarcely entered it when a gracefully dressed lady of perhaps thirty-five came towards me. I would never have taken her for the maid had she not herself made it clear to me by saying, 'The mistress is still in bed, she will come in a moment.' A bell rang, and she ran into the neighbouring room, where the bed of the goddess was, while I was left to warm myself at the fireplace, gazing first at a Danae painted on the ceiling, then at the prints which covered all the walls, and then at some French novels scattered here and there. Meanwhile the doors opened, and I felt the air was suddenly perfumed with a thousand quintessences, and I saw my fine lady, all soft and dewy, enter very quickly and almost numb with cold, and throw herself down on an easy chair which the maid had placed near the fire for her. She greeted me only with her eyes, and asked me with a smile if I had forgotten my promise. I meanwhile was handing her the book, and I noticed with wonder that she was dressed only in a thin long gown which, being unlaced, almost grazed the carpet. It left her shoulders and her breast bare, but they were voluptuously protected by a white fur which she had wrapped round her. Her hair, although it was held in place by a comb, revealed that she had recently been asleep, because some of her locks rested in ringlets on her neck, and some on her breast, as if those few black tresses were to serve as guides to inexpert eyes, and others, falling down across her forehead, obstructed her vision. She meanwhile raised her fingers to push them to one side and at times to roll them up and settle them more tidily in the comb. And as she raised her hand to do this, perhaps absent-mindedly, her gown slipped above her elbow, revealing a white and rounded arm. Resting on a little throne of cushions, she turned with pleasure to her little lapdog which came closer to her, then fled, arching its back and shaking its ears and its tail as it ran away. I sat down on a seat brought up by the maid who, by now, had vanished. That fawning little beast was now whining and gnawing, disarranging with its paws, as though deliberately, the hem of her gown, revealing a delicate silk slipper in pale pink, and then soon afterwards a little foot, O Lorenzo, such as Albani would paint on a Grace issuing from her bath. Oh! If you had, as I did, seen Teresa in the same attitude, at a fireside, having also just jumped out of bed, also en déshabillé, just as she was – calling to mind that happy morning, I remember that I would not have dared to breathe the air around her, and all my thoughts were only of worshipping her in reverence and awe – and certainly a good angel brought Teresa's image to my mind, because, I don't know how, but I managed to look at the little dog with a cautious smile, and the beautiful lady, and the little dog once more, and once again at the carpet where the pretty foot was resting. But the pretty foot had in the meantime disappeared. I arose, begging her pardon for coming at the wrong time, and as I left she was, yes, almost repentant. From being bright and courteous she had become rather sedate – but I am not sure. When I was alone my reason, which is always struggling with this heart of mine, kept saying to me, 'Wretch! You are only troubled by that beauty which has something heavenly in it: so make up your mind, and don't curl your lips at the antidote which chance offers you.' I praised my reason, but my heart had already acted according to its nature.

You will notice that this letter is a fair copy, because I wished to display *lo bello stilo*[6].

Oh, that little song of Sappho's! I hum it as I write, as I walk, as I read. I did not rave like this, Teresa, before I was prevented from seeing you and hearing you. Never mind! Eleven miles and I would be at home. And then another two miles. And then? How many times I would have fled from this region, if the fear that my misfortunes would drag me away too far from you had not kept me here in such great danger! Here we are at least under the same sky.

P.S. I have just received your letters. And once again (it must be the fifth time now, Lorenzo) you are treating me as though I were in love. Yes, I am in love, and what follows? I have seen many people fall in love with the Venus de' Medici, with Psyche, and even with the moon and with some favourite stars of theirs. And you yourself were not so enamoured of Sappho that you professed to see her portrayed in the most beautiful lady whom you knew, regarding as malignant and ignorant those who depicted her as small, dark, and rather ugly!

Joking apart, I know I am eccentric, and perhaps even odd, but should I therefore be ashamed? Of what? For some days you have been trying to put into my head the notion of blushing, but, if you will allow me to say so, I cannot, I am not able, I ought not to blush for anything in respect of Teresa, nor regret, nor lament anything. My best wishes to you!

Padua, –
From this letter two sheets have been lost. In them Jacopo tells of a spot of bother caused by his impetuous nature and his straightforward conduct. The editor, having once decided to publish the autograph scrupulously, believes it right to include here all that survives of the letter, particularly since from this it is possible to infer what is missing.

The first sheet is missing.

. . . .
. . . .
. . . .thankful for the benefits, I am

more than thankful for the insults too. Nevertheless, you know how many times I have overlooked them. I have helped those who have offended me, and sometimes I have pitied him who has betrayed me. But wounds inflicted on my honour, Lorenzo! They had to be avenged. I do not know what they may have written to you, nor do I care to know. But when that villain appeared before me, although I had not seen him for almost three years, I felt my whole body blazing. And yet I restrained myself. But did he have to exacerbate my old anger with fresh gibes? That day I felt like a lion, and I think I would have torn him to pieces, even if I had found him in the sanctuary.

Two days later the coward shunned the way of honour which I had shown him, and they all cried out for a crusade against me, as if I ought to have quietly swallowed an insult from him, who, in former times, had almost eaten my heart away. This gallant rabble affects generosity, because they all lack the courage to take a barefaced revenge, but if you saw the daggers in the night, the calumnies, and the intrigues! Besides, I didn't browbeat him. I said to him, 'You have arms and a chest as I have, and I am mortal like you.' He wept and cried, and then that overpowering anger, that fury of mine began to calm down, because his humiliation made me realise that courage does not have the right to oppress the weak. But should the weak therefore provoke him who knows how to take revenge? Believe me: it takes either vile stupidity or superhuman philosophy to leave yourself at the mercy of an enemy who has an impudent face, a black soul, and a trembling hand.

Meanwhile the affair has unmasked for me all those squires who swore me deepest friendship, who marvelled at every word of mine, and who were all the time offering me their purses and their hearts. Whited sepulchres! Beautiful marble and high-flown epitaphs: but open them up, and you find worms and a stench. Do you think, Lorenzo, that if we were reduced to begging for our bread, there would be one mindful of his promises? There would be no one, or only some shrewd ones who with their kindness wanted to purchase our humiliation. Fair-weather friends, who in a storm leave you to drown. For such people everything is basically a matter of calculation. So that if there is someone who is moved by generous passions, either he must choke them to death, or take refuge like the eagles and the nobler beasts in inaccessible mountains and forests far from men's envy and revenge. A lofty soul is so far above the multitude that they, affronted by its grandeur, try to chain it or deride it, and give the name of madness to those actions which they, sunk in their mire, can hardly recognise, much less respect. I am not speaking of myself, but when I consider the obstacles which society places in the way of genius and the heart of man, and how under licentious or tyrannical governments all is intrigue, self-interest, and calumny – I fall on my knees and thank Nature for endowing me with a temperament which cannot bear servitude, enabling me to overcome ill fortune and rise above my early influences. I know that the most valuable and only true knowledge is that of mankind, which cannot be learned in solitude, or from books. And I know that everyone should take advantage of his own good fortune, or that of others, to walk with some support along life's precipices. So be it: I myself am wary of being deceived by anyone who might edify me, hurled down by that same chance which could raise me, and beaten by the hand with the strength to support me...

Another sheet is missing.

. . . .
. . . .
. . . .if I were inexperienced, but I have experienced all the fiercest passions, and I cannot boast that I have not been tainted by any vice. It is true, no vice has ever conquered me, and on my earthly pilgrimage I have passed suddenly from a garden into a desert, but at the same time I admit that my acts of amendment were born out of a certain proud disdain, and out of despair of finding that glory and happiness for which from my earliest years I had yearned. If I had sold my faith, repudiated the truth, prostituted my brains, do you not think I would have lived to be more honoured and tranquil? But are the honours and tranquillity of my depraved century worth gaining at the expense of my soul? More than love of virtue perhaps, the fear of degradation has at times kept me from those faults which are respected in the powerful, tolerated in most people, but punished in the wretched, so that the appearance of justice may not be left without its victims. No, neither human force nor divine bullying will

ever make me play the part of the petty villain in the theatre of the world. It is, as I know well, expedient to profess oneself a libertine, staying up late in the boudoirs of our most famous beauties, because they wish to keep a good reputation where there is still some suspicion of chastity. And there were some who indoctrinated me in the arts of seduction, and encouraged me to be treacherous – and perhaps I might have betrayed and seduced, but the pleasure which I was hoping for from this turned bitter within my heart, which has never managed to be reconciled with the times or to ally itself with reason. However, you have often heard me exclaim that *everything depends on the heart!* On the heart, which neither heaven nor earth, nor our own best interests, can ever change.

In the more cultured parts of Italy, and in some French cities, I have looked eagerly for the *beau monde* which I heard praised so much. But everywhere I have found a mob of nobles, a mob of literary people, a mob of beauties, and all stupid, low, malicious – all of them. Meanwhile those few who, neglected by others and meditating in solitude, keep their distinctive characters still untouched, have escaped my notice. Meanwhile I was running here, there, and everywhere like those souls whose lives were so futile that Dante banished them from his *Hell*, not considering them worthy to be with the truly damned. In the course of a whole year do you know what I gained? Tittle-tattle, abuse, and deadly boredom. And here, from where I was looking at the past in fear and trembling, and was reassured, believing myself to be in a safe haven, the devil is dragging me off into the same troubles. Now you see how I ought to turn my eyes to the ray of hope which heaven has vouchsafed me. But I implore you, forbear to give me the usual sermon: *Jacopo, Jacopo! This recalcitrance of yours will make you misanthropic.* Do you think that, if I hated men, I would complain as I do of their vices? All the same, since I cannot laugh at them, and am afraid of being corrupted, I think it is best to retreat. And who will protect me from the hatred of this race of men so different from myself? It is useless to argue over who is right in this. I do not know, and I do not pretend that reason is all on my side. The point is (and you are at one with me here) that my proud, firm, loyal – or rather ill-mannered, stubborn, rash – disposition and the pious etiquette which dresses all the external usages of those people in one uniform, do not go together, and I certainly am not in the mood to change my clothes. And so I have no hope of a truce even, or rather I am engaged in open war, and defeat is imminent, because I cannot even fight under the cover of dissimulation, a *virtue* of much credit and even greater profit. You see my presumption! I think I am not so nasty as others are and therefore scorn to wear a disguise; or rather, whether I am good or bad, I have the greatness of soul, or if you like the impudence, to appear naked, almost as I was when I came from Nature's hands. And if, at times, I say to myself, 'Do you think the truth is any less foolhardy because it comes out of your mouth?', my conclusion is that I would be mad if, once having found in my solitude the peace of the blessed who are imparadised in the contemplation of the supreme good, I relied, in order *not to be at risk of falling in love* (your usual litany), on the judgement of this ceremonious and malign riff-raff.

This godforsaken place puts me to sleep. I am bored with living. You may reprove me as much as you like, but in Padua I don't know what to do with myself. If you could only see my sulky face now, and see me idling, hardly able to begin this paltry letter! Teresa's father has come back to the hills and has written to me. I have replied, letting him know that we shall see each other again before long, and to me it seems like a thousand years.

This university (probably like most of the universities in the world, unfortunately) is for the most part composed of proud professors at odds with each other, and dissolute students. Do you know why outstanding men are so rare among the horde of learned ones? This instinct imparted from on high, which makes a genius what he is, can only survive in independence and solitude, when the times prevent him from acting and leave him with nothing but writing. In society we read much, we do not meditate, and we imitate each other. Since we are always talking, that generous rage which makes us feel, think, and write powerfully, simply evaporates. Through babbling in many languages, we end up babbling also in our own, ridiculous at once to strangers and to ourselves. Dependent on the interests, the prejudices, and the vices of the men among whom we live, and controlled by a string of duties and needs, we commit our glory and our happiness to the multitude. We finger riches and power, and we even fear to be great because fame incites persecution, and high-mindedness makes governments suspicious: rulers want men who will never be either heroes or illustrious villains. And therefore those who in servile times are paid to teach, seldom or never lay down their lives for the truth or for the inviolability of the academy. Hence that display of professorial lectures which make reasoning difficult and truth suspect. On the other hand I suspect that men are all as blind as one another. They travel in the dark, and some of them contrive to open their eyes, imagining that they can make things out in the darkness through which they have to grope their way. But forget what I have said: there are some opinions which should be discussed only with those few who scoff at knowledge as Homer scoffed at the valour of the frogs and the mice.

By the way, will you please listen to me just for once? Now that God has provided a buyer, sell all my books, body and soul. What do I need with more than four thousand volumes which I cannot and do not wish to read? Keep those few which you find have marginal annotations in my hand. Oh, I used to spend all my time and money on books! Now that madness has left me, but only to give place to another. Let my mother have the proceeds. It seems the quickest way to reimburse her for all my expenses – but how to recompense her? Truly, I would give her an entire treasure. The times are getting even more calamitous, and it is not right that that poor lady should, for my sake, be in difficulties for what remains of her life. Farewell.

FROM THE EUGANEAN HILLS, 3RD JANUARY 1798
Forgive me, but I thought you were wiser. The human race is that herd of blind men you see colliding with each other, thrusting themselves forward, fighting, and running to meet, or being dragged along behind, their inexorable fate. So what is the point of pursuing, or fearing, what is bound to happen?

Am I wrong? Can human prudence break this invisible chain of chances and numberless tiny events which we call destiny? Perhaps, but can it therefore give us a clear view of the future which lies in shadow? Oh! Once more you exhort me to flee from Teresa, and that is as much as to say, 'Abandon what makes life precious to you, avoid one trouble, and fall into something worse.' Suppose that, out of a prudent fear of danger, I closed my mind to every gleam of happiness. Would not all my life then be rather like the harsh days of this foggy season, which make us wish not to exist while Nature is so afflicted? Tell the truth, Lorenzo. Would it not be better if part, at least, of the morning were comforted by the rays of the sun, even if this meant that night carried off the day before evening? If I had to keep a constant watch on my irrepressible heart, I would always be at war with myself, and to no advantage. I shall give myself up for lost, and let what happens happen. Meanwhile:

> *I feel the ancient breeze, see with delight*
> *Those hills once more...*[7]

10TH JANUARY

Odoardo hopes to have his affairs sorted out in a month. He has written to say this, so he will return at the latest in spring. Well then, towards the first of April I think it will be sensible for me to leave.

19TH JANUARY

Human life? A dream, a deceptive dream which we value so very highly, just as foolish women entrust their future to superstitions and presentiments! Think on this: what you reach out for so greedily is perhaps a shadow, dear to you, but wearisome to someone else. Well then, all my happiness is in the empty appearances of the things which now surround me, and if I look for something which is real, either I deceive myself once more, or I wander dumbfounded and frightened through nothingness! I don't know, but I suspect that Nature made our species just about the tiniest ineffectual link in her incomprehensible system, giving us so much self-love to ensure that the great fear and hope which fill our imaginations with an infinite series of ills and blessings, keep us always troubled about this short, uncertain, unhappy existence of ours. And while we blindly serve her ends, she laughs at our pride that makes us consider that the universe was made for us alone, and that we alone are worthy and capable of giving laws to creation.

Earlier today I went for a wander through the countryside, with my cloak pulled up to my eyes, pondering the bleakness of the earth buried under the snow, without grass or leaves to remind me of its former richness. Nor could my eyes bear to look for long at the shoulders of the mountains, their summits bathed in a black cloud of frozen mist which hung there to augment the appearance of mourning in the cold and overcast air. And I seemed to see those snows melt and plunge down in torrents flooding the plain, dragging headlong with them plants, herds, and huts, and ending in one day the labours of so many years, and the hopes of so many families. From time to time a ray of sunlight made its way through and, although it was soon overcome by the fog, led me to believe that only thanks to that ray itself was the world not sunk in one deep perpetual night. And I, turning to that part of the sky which was still white with the traces of the sun's splendour, said, 'O Sun, everything changes here below! And the day will come when God will withdraw his countenance from you, and you too will be transformed. Then will the clouds no more woo your declining rays, nor will dawn, garlanded with celestial roses and circled by your rays, come in the east to announce that you are rising. Meanwhile, enjoy your course, which may well be a labour to you, as man's is to him. You can see it: man does not enjoy his days, and if at times it is given to him to walk through the flowering April meadows, he must still fear also the blazing air of summer, and the deadly ice of winter.'

22ND JANUARY

So it goes, dear friend. I was standing at my steward's hearth, where some of the neighbouring peasants gather to warm up, to pass on news and recount their old experiences. A girl came in, barefoot and frozen, and she asked the gardener for alms for some poor old woman. While she was taking some refreshment at the fire, he got two bundles of wood ready for her, and two loaves of brown bread. The girl seized them, said goodbye to us, and went out. I too went out and, without realising, I followed her, treading in her footprints in the snow. When she came to a heap of ice, she stopped to examine another path, and I caught up with her. 'Are you going far?' I asked her. 'No sir, half a mile.' 'But you are finding it hard to walk with those two bundles. Let me carry one of them.' 'The bundles wouldn't bother me so much if I could hold them on my shoulder with both arms, but these two loaves are getting in my way.' 'Right then, I'll carry the loaves.' She didn't breathe a word. She went red, and she handed me the loaves which I put under my cloak. After a short time we came to a little hovel and went in. In one corner a little old woman was sitting. Between her feet was a brazier filled with dying embers over which she was holding out her palms, while her wrists rested on her bent knees. 'Good day, mother.' 'Good day.' 'How are you, mother?' Neither to this nor to a dozen other questions could I manage to get a reply. She was intent on warming her hands, raising her eyes now and then as if to see whether or not we had left. Meanwhile we put the few provisions down, and the old woman, without looking at us again, sat looking at them, her eyes unmoving, and to our goodbyes and our promises to return the next day she replied only with another reluctant, 'Good-day.'

On the way home the girl told me how that woman, despite her eighty or more years and her hard circumstances (it happened sometimes that storms prevented the countryfolk from bringing the alms they had gathered for her, so that she was on the point of dying from hunger), was nevertheless always in fear and trembling of death and mumbling prayers for heaven to keep her alive. I then heard from old people of the district that many years ago her husband had died from a harquebus shot, and that she had had sons and daughters, and then sons-in-law, daughters-in law, and grandchildren, all of whom she had seen perish and fall round her in the memorable year of the great hunger. And yet, my friend, neither her past nor her present misfortunes have killed her, and she still has some hold on life while struggling in a sea of troubles.

Ah well! So many troubles besiege our life that preserving it requires nothing less than an overwhelming blind instinct which (however easy Nature makes the ways to free us from it) often forces us to purchase it with humiliation, with tears, and sometimes even with crimes!

For two months you have had no sign of life from me, and you are dismayed – and you fear that I am, by now, so overwhelmed by love that I forget both you and my native land. Lorenzo, my friend, you know little of me and the human heart, or of yourself, if you think that my solicitude for my native land could ever weaken, much less be extinguished, if you believe that it gives place to other passions. It does provoke other passions, and is provoked by them. It is true indeed, and in this you say well: *Love in an embittered heart, and where the other passions are in despair, becomes all-powerful.* And I am evidence of this. But you are wrong if you think it proves disastrous. Without Teresa, I would perhaps today be dead and buried.

On her own initiative Nature creates some minds that cannot be other than magnanimous. Twenty years ago such minds stayed frozen and inert in the general stupor of Italy, but these present times have reawakened their native manly passions, and they have been so tempered that you may break them but never bend them. And this is not an abstruse notion: it is a truth which shines out from the lives of many ancient mortals who were gloriously unhappy, a truth I have verified by living among many of our fellow citizens. And I admire them and pity them at the same time, because, if God has no pity on Italy, they will have to keep secret their desire for a homeland – a fatal desire because it either consumes or brings suffering to one's whole life. And yet, rather than abandon this desire, they will cherish the dangers, the anguish, and death itself. And I am one of these men, and so are you, Lorenzo.

But if I wrote about what I have seen and learned of our affairs, I would be doing something unnecessary and cruel, reawakening in you all the rage which I would rather appease within myself. Believe me, I do weep for our homeland. I weep in secret, and I desire 'simply to shed some solitary tears.'[8]

Let other lovers of Italy complain at the tops of their voices. They cry out that they have been sold and betrayed. But if they had taken up arms, they might have been conquered, yet not betrayed, and if they had defended themselves to the last drop of blood, the conquerors could not have sold them, nor the conquered dared to buy them. But many of us believe that liberty can be bought with money. They believe that foreign nations come out of love of justice to slaughter and be slaughtered on our fields in order to liberate Italy! But will the French – they who have made the divine name of human liberty abominable – act like Timoleon on our behalf? Many meanwhile trust in the Young Hero[9] born of Italian stock, born where they speak our language. I myself shall never expect anything good or exalted from a base and cruel mind. What does it matter that he has the strength and roar of a lion, if he has the mind of a fox and is glad to have it? Yes, base and cruel – those adjectives are not exaggerated. Why did he not sell Venice openly and with a noble ferocity? Selim I, who ordered the slaughter on the Nile of thirty thousand Circassian soldiers who had surrendered on his promise of mercy, and Shah Nadir, who in our century slaughtered three hundred thousand Indians, committed greater atrocities, but are less contemptible. I saw with my own eyes a democratic constitution annotated by the Young Hero, annotated in his hand, sent from Passeriano to Venice to be accepted, and the Treaty of Campoformio had already been signed, and Venice sold, several days previously. And the trust which the Hero encouraged all of us to have in him has resulted in proscriptions in Italy, emigration, and exile. I do not complain of reasons of state which lead nations to be sold like flocks of sheep. So it always was, and so it always will be. I mourn for my homeland, taken from me, '*in a way that still offends*.'[10]

He was born an Italian, and one day he will bring succour to his homeland. Others may believe this if they like, but I have replied, and always shall reply that *Nature made him a tyrant, and a tyrant does not take care of his homeland, because he has none*.

Some others of us, seeing Italy's wounds, are, however, preaching that those wounds must be healed by extreme measures, necessary for our liberty. Now it is true that Italy has clerics and monks, but not priests, because where religion is not involved in the laws and customs of a people, the administration of the rituals is merely business. Italy has as many nobles as you like, but she has not really any patricians, because patricians with one hand defend the republic in war, and with the other hand govern it in peace. And in Italy the proudest boast of the nobles is that they do nothing and never know anything. Finally we come to the populace. They are not really citizens – or few of them are. The doctors, the lawyers, the university professors, the men of letters, the rich merchants, the innumerable swarm of workmen say that they perform noble and civil tasks, but they do not have civil power and rights. Whoever earns his bread, or his wealth, by his own toil, and does not own land, is no more than one of the populace – less wretched, but no less servile. There can be land without inhabitants, but a people without land, never. For this reason the few country squires in Italy will always be the invisible lords and arbiters of the nation. Now let us make priests out of clerics and monks, patricians out of nobles, well-to-do citizens and landed gentry out of the lower classes, or at least out of most of them. But make sure that it be without massacres, without sacrilegious reforms in religion, without factions, without proscriptions and banishments, without the aid and the blood and the depredations of foreign arms, without dividing up the lands, without agrarian laws, without the seizure of family properties. For if, as I believe and always have believed, if these remedies were ever necessary to free us from our notorious perpetual servitude, I myself do not know what I would choose – not infamy, and not servitude. I would not even put into execution such cruel and often inefficacious remedies – but the individual has yet many roads to safety… if nothing else, the grave – but a whole nation cannot be buried. Therefore, if I were to write, I would exhort Italy to accept her present state peacefully, leaving to France the misfortune and the disgrace of having for the sake of liberty bled so many human victims dry – on whom the tyranny of the five, or of the five hundred, or of one alone (they all come to the same thing) has planted or will plant its throne, wobbling from minute to minute, like all those thrones which are founded upon dead bodies…

The long time which has gone by since I wrote to you has not been time lost to me. Rather, I think I have gained too much – and fatally so! Signor T*** has many volumes of political philosophy and of the best historians of the modern world; and partly through not wishing to be near Teresa too often, and partly through boredom and curiosity – two states which often incite human beings to action – I had those books sent to me, and some I have read, and some I have riffled through, and they have been sad companions for me this winter. Certainly I thought I had more lovable companions among the little birds which, driven by the cold to look in desperation for food near the homes of men, their enemies, alighted in families and tribes on my balcony where I put something out for their lunch and dinner. But perhaps now that their need is less they will not visit me any more. Meanwhile, from my lengthy reading I have gathered that not being acquainted with men is a dangerous thing. But knowing them when one does not wish to deceive them is fatal! I have gathered that the many opinions to be found in our books, and their historical contradictions, lead one to Pyrrhonism and send one wandering off in confusion, in chaos, in nothingness: so that, if I were forced to read all the time, or not to read ever, I would opt for never reading. And maybe I shall do that. I have gathered that we all have futile passions, like the vanity of life itself, and that nevertheless such vanity is the source of our errors, our grief, and our crimes.

Yet I feel that this passion of mine for a homeland is increasing all the time. And when I think of Teresa – and if I begin to hope – I suddenly come back to myself with greater consternation than before, and I say again, 'Even if my friend were the mother of my children, my children would not have a homeland, and the dear companion of my life would to her sorrow realise it.' It is only too true! To the other passions which make girls, and especially Italian girls, sorrow at the dawning of their brief day, is added this unhappy love of their homeland. I have distracted Signor T*** from political discussions, which he loves. His daughter never opened her mouth, yet I noticed nevertheless that her father's troubles and mine were entering into that girl's heart. You know that she is not an ordinary young woman, and even apart from her concerns – since in other times she would have been able to choose another husband – she is gifted with a proud mind and with refined thoughts. And she sees how burdensome to me is this gloomy, cold, and egotistical idleness in which I waste all my days – truly, Lorenzo, even when I am silent, I show how wretched and base I am in my own eyes. A strong will and a lack of power make anyone who feels political passion miserable within, and they make him appear ridiculous in the eyes of the world, if he does not stay silent. He becomes the figure of a knight in a romance, the impotent lover of his own city. When Cato killed himself, a wretched patrician called Cotius followed suit. The former was admired because he had at first tried every way to avoid being reduced to subjection; the latter was laughed at because his love of liberty left him with nothing to do but kill himself.

But being here, near Teresa – in my thoughts at least, because I still have such self-control that I let three or four days go by without seeing her – the mere remembrance makes me feel a soothing fire, a light, a consolation for my life – short perhaps, but a heavenly sweetness – and so for the moment I am preserved from absolute desperation.

And when I am with her – of someone else you would perhaps not credit it, but you would of me – well then, I do not speak to her of love. It is now half a year since her soul was united with mine, and she has never heard anything from my lips to make her certain that I love her. But how could she not be certain? Her father spends whole evenings playing chess with me. She sits working at that table nearby, in silence except when her eyes speak, which is seldom, and then they immediately look down, asking me only for compassion.

And how can I ever show my compassion, except by keeping hidden, hidden from her, all my passions as far as I am able? I live for her alone. And when this new sweet dream of mine ends too, I shall be glad to let the curtain fall on my life. Glory, knowledge, youth, riches, homeland, all the fancies that up to now have had parts in my comedy, no longer mean anything to me. I shall let the curtain fall, and I shall leave it to other mortals to worry about increasing the pleasures and lessening the pains of a life which is growing shorter by the minute, and which those wretches would like to believe is everlasting.

And so in my usual disorderly way, but with unusual placidity, I have replied to your long affectionate letter. You are better able to say what you think – I feel things too much, and so I seem stubborn. But if I listened more to others than to myself, I would perhaps be annoyed with myself – and not being annoyed with himself is the one slight happiness which a man can hope for on this earth.

3RD APRIL

When the soul is wholly absorbed in a sort of beatitude, our feeble faculties, overwhelmed with such great pleasure, become stunned, mute, and unable to cope with any task. So if I were not living the life of a saint, you would get letters from me more often. If misfortunes make our lives more burdensome, we rush to impart them to some unhappy person, and he wrings some comfort from knowing that he is not the only one in tears. But if some moments of happiness shine out, we concentrate them all in ourselves, for fear that our good fortune would diminish if it were shared. Or else our pride alone leads us to boast of it. And then that man does not feel his passion deeply, whether it be happy or sad, who is able to describe it so minutely.

Meanwhile Nature is returning in her beauty – as she must have been when, coming to life in the beginning from the formless abyss of Chaos, she sent the smiling April dawn out as a harbinger. And she, loosening her blond hair in the east, and then little by little clothing the universe in her rosy mantle, spread the propitious dews around, and roused the virginal breath of the breezes to announce – to the flowers, to the clouds, to the waves, and to all the beings which were greeting her – the sun... the sun, the heavenly image of God, light, soul, life of all creation!

6TH APRIL

It is true, only too true! My fantasy conjures up so realistically the happiness which I desire, and holds it before my eyes, and I am about to touch it with my hand, and I have only a few steps to go – and then? My sad heart sees it fade away, and I weep as if I were losing a blessing which I had long possessed.

However, Odoardo writes to her that the legal imbroglio was at first the reason for his delay, and that then the revolution has interrupted legal proceedings for several days. One might add that where interest predominates, the other passions are subdued. A new love perhaps... But you will say, 'What does all that matter?' It doesn't matter, Lorenzo. God forbid that I should take advantage of Odoardo's coldness. But I don't know how anyone could stay away from her a day longer! Shall I therefore continue to entertain illusions, only in order to gulp down afterwards the fatal draught which I myself have prepared?

11TH APRIL

She was seated on a sofa opposite the window from which one can see the hills, looking at the clouds sauntering across the wide expanse of sky. 'Notice,' she said to me, 'that deep blue.' I stood near her, utterly silent, my eyes fixed on her hand which was holding a little book half open. I don't know why, but I failed to notice that the storm was beginning to growl from the north, and was knocking down the younger plants. 'Those poor saplings!' cried Teresa. I started. The shades of night were thickening, and the lightning made the night seem even blacker. The rain came pouring down, and there was thunder. Shortly afterwards I saw the windows were shut and the lamps lit in the room. The servant boy, doing what he was accustomed to do every evening and expecting bad weather, had come to snatch away from us the spectacle of Nature in her rage. And Teresa, who was lost in thought, did not notice it and let him carry on.

I took the book from her hand and, opening it at random, I read:

Tender Glyceria has left her last sigh upon these lips of mine. With Glyceria I have lost all that I ever could lose. Her grave is the only bit of land which I deign to call mine. No one but me knows where it is. I have covered it with dense rose bushes which bloom as once her face bloomed, and diffuse the sweet fragrance which exhaled from her breast. Every year in the month of roses I visit the sacred grove. I sit upon that mound of earth which covers her bones. I pluck a rose, and I think, 'Just as you flourished once!' And I pull the petals from that rose and scatter them, and I recall that sweet dream of love that was ours. O my Glyceria, where are you? A tear falls on the grass which grows on the tomb, and appeases the loving shade.

I fell silent. 'Why aren't you reading?' she asked, looking at me and sighing. I read the passage again, and when I reached *Just as you flourished once!* my voice choked. A tear from Teresa dropped on my hand which was clasping hers.

17TH APRIL

Do you remember that young girl who was on holiday four years ago at the foot of these hills? She was the sweetheart of our friend Olivo P***, and you know how he was reduced to poverty and could not have her for his bride? Today I saw her again, married off to a nobleman, a relative of the T*** family. While she was passing through her lands, she visited Teresa. I was sitting on the carpet there, very attentive to the copy work of my little Isabella, who sat on a chair scribbling her ABCs. When I saw her, I immediately rose and ran towards her as if to embrace her. But how changed she was! Sedate, refined, she found it difficult to recognise me, showed her surprise, and then muttered a greeting, half to me, half to Teresa. I am sure that the unexpected sight of me had disconcerted her. But, chatting about jewels and ribbons and necklaces and bonnets, she became more at ease. I hoped to do her a good turn by diverting the conversation from such trifles, and because almost all young girls' faces become more beautiful and have no need of other ornaments when they speak modestly and from the heart, I reminded her of the happy days she had spent in that countryside. 'Yes, yes,' she replied absently, and then she went on anatomising the foreign *beau travail* of her earrings. Her husband meanwhile (because among the *giant race of the pigmies* he has scrounged fame as a *savant*, like Algarotti and ***) was studding his perfect Tuscan speech with a thousand phrases of French, and extolling the value of those trifles, and his bride's good taste. I was about to pick up my hat, but a glance from Teresa stopped me. The conversation gradually came round to the books we were reading in the country. Then you might have heard his lordship singing the praises of the *prodigious* library of his ancestors, and the collection of all the *editiones principes* of the ancients which in his travels he had taken the trouble to *complete*. I smiled to myself, while he continued with his disquisition on title-pages. In the Lord's good time a servant, who had gone in search of Signor T***, returned and informed Teresa that he had not been able to find him because he had gone into the mountains to hunt, and the disquisition was broken off. I asked the new bride about Olivo, because I had not seen him again after his misfortunes. You can imagine how I felt when I heard his former lover say coldly, 'He is dead.' 'Dead,' I exclaimed, leaping to my feet, and goggling at her stupefied. And I described to Teresa the outstanding character of that peerless young man, and the bad luck which forced him to struggle with poverty and disgrace; and that he died without stain or spot.

Well, now the husband started to tell us of the death of Olivo's father, the dissension between him and his elder brother, the quarrels which became ever more bitter, and the decision of the courts which, adjudicating between two sons of the same father, enriched one by impoverishing the other. What little remained to poor Olivo was eaten up by legal fees. He moralised over this *eccentric* young man who refused his brother's help, and instead of trying to be reconciled with him, embittered him still more. 'Yes, yes,' I replied, 'if his brother could not be just, then Olivo ought not to have been base. He is a wretch who will not listen to the counsels and compassion of friendship, and scorns reciprocal sighs of sympathy, and refuses ready help at the hand of a friend. But a thousand times more wretched is he who trusts in the friendship of the rich, and taking virtue for granted in him who never knew misfortune, accepts that benefit which he will then have to pay for with the loss of so much integrity. Happiness never associates itself with misfortune except to buy gratitude and tyrannise over virtue. Man, an oppressive creature, takes advantage of fortune's caprices to give himself the right to triumph. Only the afflicted can help and console one another without offence, but he who comes to the table of the rich man, soon (but even then too late) realises:

> '… *how bitter is the taste*
> *Of strangers' bread.*'[11]

And so, how much less grievous it is to go from door to door cadging one's bread than be humiliated, and loathe the indiscreet benefactor who, parading his charity, demands in return your blushes and your liberty!'

'But,' the husband replied, 'you did not let me finish. Since Olivo left his father's house, renouncing all his claims in favour of his elder brother, *why* did he want to pay his father's debts? What? Did he himself not go to meet poverty, mortgaging through this foolish scrupulosity even his own portion of his mother's dowry?'

'Why? The heir defrauded the creditors by legal subterfuges. But is that a reason for Olivo to allow his father's bones to be cursed by those who in adversity had come to his aid with their own substance, and for he himself to be pointed at in the streets as the son of bankrupt? This high-minded honesty discredited his brother who was not inclined to imitate it, and who after vainly trying to tempt his brother with help, swore to him an enmity that was deadly, despotic, and fraternal. Meanwhile Olivo lost the help of those who were perhaps praising him in private, because he had been outdone by rogues, since it is easier to approve virtue than support it with all one's might and follow it. That is why a decent man among evil people is always ruined, and why we always join forces with the stronger, trample on him who is on the ground, and judge after seeing the outcome.'

No one replied to this. They were perhaps beaten in argument, but certainly not persuaded. And I added, 'Rather than mourn Olivo, I thank the good Lord who has called him away from such wickedness and from our idiocy. Because, to tell the truth, we ourselves, we devotees of virtue, are also idiots! There are certain men who need death, because they cannot get used to the crimes of the wicked or the pusillanimity of good men.'

The bride seemed moved. 'It is only too true,' she exclaimed with a sigh. 'But on the other hand he who lacks bread must not be too particular about his honour.'

'And this is another of your absurdities!' I burst out. 'Because you are favoured by fortune, you would like to be the only honest people. Or is it rather that, since virtue does not shine in your dark souls, you would drive it from the breasts of those who are unfortunate, although they have no other comfort, hoping in this way to beguile your consciences?' With her eyes Teresa said that I was right, although she was anxious to change the subject. But there was no stopping me. And how could I remain silent? Now I do feel some remorse for what I said: the eyes of the married couple were looking down, and their souls were cast down too, when I cried out boldly, 'Those who have never been unfortunate are not worthy of their happiness. How proud they are! They look at misery only to insult it. They think that everything ought to offer itself as a tribute to wealth and pleasure. But the unfortunate man who keeps his dignity is a sight that encourages the good, and reproaches the wicked.'

Then I went out, running my fingers through my hair. I am grateful to the early misfortunes in my life which made me one of the unlucky

43

ones! Otherwise, Lorenzo, I might not now be your friend, or might not be the friend of this girl. What happened this morning is still in my mind. Here where I am sitting by myself, I look around and fear that I may see one of my acquaintances. Who would ever have thought it? Her heart did not quiver at the name of her first love. She even dared to disturb the ashes of him who for the first time inspired her with the universal feeling for life. Not a single sigh? 'But you are mad,' I tell myself, 'and you're upset because you do not find among men that virtue which is perhaps, yes, perhaps only an empty name – or a necessity which changes according to passions and circumstances – or a natural arrogance in some few individuals who, having generous and merciful dispositions, must wage perpetual war against the mass of mankind. If only that were all! But woe betide them when, whether they want to or not, they have to open their eyes to the mournful light of disenchantment!'

I am not naturally morose, as you well know, Lorenzo. In my early youth I wanted to scatter flowers on the heads of all living things. What else has made me so touchy and severe to the greater part of mankind but their hypocritical cruelty? I would be willing to pardon all the wrongs that have been done to me. But when I think of honourable poverty struggling while its veins are sucked dry by omnipotent opulence, and when I see so many sick, imprisoned, hungry people all suppliants beneath the dreadful lash of certain laws – no, I cannot be reconciled to this. No, I cry vengeance together with those wretches whose bread and tears I share. And I make bold to ask back, on their behalf, the portion which is their inheritance from Nature, our benevolent and impartial mother. But Nature, our mother? If she has arranged everything like this, is she not rather our wicked stepmother?

Yes, Teresa, I shall live where you are, but I shall only live as long as I can live where you are. You are one of those few angels scattered here and there upon the face of the earth to make people believe in virtue, and inspire persecuted and afflicted minds with a love of humanity. But if I were to lose you, what way out would there be for this young man who is aggrieved with all the rest of the world?

If you had seen her a little while ago! She held out her hand to me, saying, 'Be discreet. They did both seem to me to be conscience-stricken, and if Olivo had not been unfortunate, would he have had someone to be a friend to him even after his death?'

Then, after a long silence, she added, 'Ah, does one have to suffer in order to love virtue?'

Lorenzo, her heavenly soul shined through the lineaments of her face!

29TH APRIL

When I am near her I am so full of life that I scarcely feel I am alive. Just as when I awaken after a peaceful sleep, if the rays of the sun shine onto my eyes, I am dazzled and cannot see for the torrent of light.

For a long time I have been lamenting the idleness in which I live. When spring came, I decided to study botany. In two weeks I had gathered on the crags several dozen plants, and now I no longer know where I put them. Many times I left my *Linnaeus* forgotten on a seat in the garden or under some trees. Now I have lost it. Yesterday Michele brought me two leaves of the book all wet with dew, and this morning he informed me that the remainder had been badly soiled by the gardener's dog.

Teresa reproaches me. To please her I set about writing, but, although I start with the best intentions, I cannot manage more than three or four sentences. A thousand arguments occur to me, a thousand ideas appear before me. I choose, I reject, and then I go back to choosing. At last I write, I tear up what I have written, I erase things, and in this way I often waste both morning and evening. My mind grows tired, my fingers let the pen drop, and I realise I have thrown away both time and effort. I have already told you that writing books is both beyond and beneath my power. If you consider also my state of mind, you will realise that, if now and then I write you a letter, that is no slight achievement. Oh, what a ridiculous figure I cut when she is sitting working and I am reading aloud! All at once I stop, and she tells me to go on. I go back to reading. After a couple of pages I start to speak more quickly and end up with a rhythmic mumbling. Teresa is troubled: 'Please read so that I can understand a little of what you're saying!' I continue, but my eyes are unwittingly distracted from the book, and they find themselves fixed upon that angelic face. I fall silent.

The book falls shut. I lose my place and cannot find it again. Teresa means to be angry, but she smiles.

If only I could grasp all the thoughts that run through my imagination! I am noting them down on the back of the cover and in the margins of my Plutarch, but no sooner are they written, than they slip out of my mind, and when I go looking for them on the page, I find abortive notions – meagre, disconnected, and frigid. What a lame expedient, to note thoughts down instead of leaving them to mature in the mind! But this is how books are written when they are a patchwork of other books. And I too, quite unintentionally, have found myself making a patchwork. In a little English book[12] I have found a disastrous tale, and at every word I felt I was reading about the misfortunes of poor Lauretta. The sun always and everywhere shines on the same woes! Now, so as not to seem idle, I have tried to write down what happened to Lauretta. By translating the tale exactly, and taking very little away from it, changing it very little, and adding very little to it of my own, I would have told the truth. Instead, my tale is nothing but fiction. Through the story of that unfortunate creature I wanted to show Teresa a mirror of the *fatal* unhappiness of love. But the maxims, the counsels, and the examples of harm done to someone else do nothing but provoke our own passions. Besides, instead of speaking about Lauretta, I have spoken about myself. Such is my state of mind that I always go back to fingering my own wounds. However, I don't think I shall let Teresa read these three or four pages. It would do her more harm than good. And for now I am even going to stop writing. You read them. Farewell.

FRAGMENT OF THE STORY OF LAURETTA

I do not know if heaven cares about the earth. Even if heaven has bothered about us occasionally (or at least on the first day when the human race started to swarm) I think that Destiny has written in her eternal books: 'Man will be unhappy'.

I dare not appeal against this sentence. I would hardly know to what court I should make my appeal. Moreover, I like to think it would be a useful thought for so many races living in all the other countless worlds. However, I am grateful to that Mind which, mingling with the universe of beings, always brings them back to life by destroying them, because, with all our miseries, that Mind has at least given us the gift of weeping, and has punished those who, made impudent by their philosophy, try to rebel against our human lot by denying us the inexhaustible pleasures of compassion. If you see someone sorrowful and weeping, do not weep. *Stoic, do you not know that the tears of a compassionate man are sweeter to the unhappy man than dew upon withered grass?*

O Lauretta! I wept with you on the bier of your poor lover, and I recall that my compassion sweetened the bitterness of your grief. You fell upon my breast, and your blond hair covered my face, and your tears bathed my cheeks. Then you dried my cheeks with your handkerchief, and dried your tears which were once more gushing from your eyes and running down onto your lips. Forsaken by everyone! But not by me. I have never abandoned you.

When you were wandering distraught along the solitary seashore, I followed stealthily in your footsteps so that I might save you from the desperation of your grief. Then I called you by name, and you held out your hand to me, and sat by my side. The moon was rising, and you gazed at it and sang piteously. Some might have presumed to jeer at you, but the comforter of the afflicted, who looks with an impartial eye on the madness and the wisdom of men, and has compassion on their crimes and their virtues, may have heard your sad words and breathed some comfort. The prayers of my heart accompanied you, and the vows and the offerings of grieving souls are acceptable to God. The waves were moaning plaintively. They were rippling in the wind, and almost lapping the beach on which we were sitting. And you arose and, leaning on my arm, made your way to that stone where you seemed to see your Eugenio once more, and hear his voice, and feel the touch of his hand, and taste his kisses. 'Now what is left for me?' you exclaimed. 'The war has taken my brothers from me, and death has seized my father and my lover. I am abandoned by everyone!'

O Beauty, beneficent spirit of nature! Where you display your lovable smile joy abounds, and delight is spread abroad to perpetuate the life of the universe. May he who does not know and appreciate you be detestable to the world and to himself. But when you are endeared by virtue, when misfortunes, which take away all boldness from you and all envy of your happiness, show you to the world bereft of cheerful garlands and with your locks unbound – oh, then who could pass by you and give you no more than a futile glance of compassion?

But I offered you, Lauretta, my tears, and this hermitage of mine where you could eat my bread, drink from my cup, and fall asleep upon my breast. Everything I had! And perhaps with me your life would have been, not joyful indeed, but at least free and peaceful. In solitude and peace the heart little by little forgets its troubles. Because peace and liberty delight in the simple and solitary nature.

One evening in autumn the moon could hardly be seen from the earth. Its rays were reflected on the thin clouds which accompanied it and covered it up from time to time, and which, scattered as they were through the expanse of the sky, snatched the stars from our sight. We gazed at the distant fires of the fishermen, and listened to the song of the gondolier whose oar disturbed the silence and calm of the dark lagoon. But Lauretta turned and looked around for her lover. And she arose, and wandered about a little calling out to him. Then she came back wearily to where I was sitting, and sat down as though she were frightened by the solitude. She looked at me and it seemed she wanted to say, 'I shall be abandoned by you too!' And she called her lapdog.

I abandon her? Who would ever have thought that that would be the last evening I would see her? She was dressed in white. Her hair was held by a sky-blue ribbon, and there were three withered violets on the centre of the linen which veiled her bosom. I accompanied her to the entrance of her home, and her mother, coming to open the door for us, thanked me for the care I had taken of her distressed daughter. When I was alone I realised that I still had her handkerchief in my hand. 'I shall give it back to her tomorrow,' I said to myself.

Her troubles were starting to diminish, and perhaps I… It is true that I could not give you your Eugenio, but I would have been husband, father, brother to you. My persecuting fellow-citizens, helped by some foreign rogues, unexpectedly proscribed me by name, and I could not, Lauretta, even bid you my last farewell.

When the future comes into my mind, and I close my eyes to it, and lose myself trembling in the memory of days that are past, I find myself wandering and wandering under the trees in this valley, and I recall the shores of the sea, and the distant fires, and the song of the gondolier. I lean upon a trunk and think, 'Heaven gave her to me, but adverse fortune has snatched her away!' I draw out her handkerchief. 'Unhappy the one whose love is mingled with ambition! But your heart, O Lauretta, was meant for one who is open-hearted.' I dry my eyes, and as night falls I return home.

And you, what are you doing now? Are you wandering along the beach again, offering your prayers and tears to God? Come! You will gather the fruits of my garden. You will drink from my cup, you will eat my bread, and you will lean upon my breast *and you will feel how my heart beats so very differently today. When your suffering returns, and you are overcome by emotion, I shall go behind you to help you along your road, make sure you do not get lost, and guide you to my home. But I shall go behind you silently and leave you free, at least, to find comfort in your tears. I shall be a father, a brother to you – but my heart, if you could see my heart!* A tear falls upon the page and smudges what I am writing.

I saw her in the bloom of youth and beauty, and then I saw her driven mad, rambling, orphaned. And I saw her kiss the dying lips of her one comforter – and then kneel in pious superstition before her mother, weeping and begging her to withdraw the curse which that wretched mother had thundered against her daughter. So poor Lauretta left me with an enduring compassion for her misfortunes. This is a precious inheritance which I would like to share with all you who are left with no comfort but your love and sympathy for virtue. You do not know me, but whoever you are, we are friends. Do not hate men who are prosperous: simply flee from them.

Have you seen how, after days of storm, the living rays of the sun break through the golden clouds in the east and comfort nature once again? That is how the sight of her is for me. I banish my desires, condemn my hopes, weep for my illusions: no, I will not see her again. I will not love her.

I hear a voice calling me traitor – the voice of her father! I am angry with myself, and I feel a saving virtue rise again in my heart – repentance. So here I am, firmly resolved, more firmly than ever. But then? When I see her face, my illusions return, and my soul is transformed, and it forgets itself, imparadised in the contemplation of beauty.

8TH MAY

She does not love you. Even if she wanted to, she cannot. It is true, Lorenzo, but if I agreed to tear this veil away from my eyes, I should have to close them straightaway in everlasting sleep, for without this angelic light, life to me would be terror, the world a chaos, Nature a desert in the night. Rather than extinguish one by one the torches which illuminate the theatrical scene, and disillusion the spectators rudely, would it not be much better to let the curtain fall suddenly, and leave them with their illusions? *But if the illusion is harmful...* Does it matter? The disillusionment would kill me!

One Sunday I heard the parish priest scolding the peasants for getting drunk. And he didn't realise that he was spoiling for these wretched people the comfort of dulling by their evening drunkenness the labours of the day, of not feeling the bitterness of earning their bread with sweat and tears, and of forgetting the harshness and hunger which the coming winter threatens.

11TH MAY

One must admit that Nature still has need of this globe and of the quarrelsome species which inhabits it. And it is to provide for everyone's preservation, rather than to bind us together in mutual friendship, that Nature has made everyone so much a friend to himself that he would happily desire the elimination of the universe if his own existence might be more secure and he himself survive as the solitary despot of all creation. No generation has ever lived its whole life in peace, war has always been the arbiter of human rights, and force has held sway over every century. So man, either openly or secretly, and always the implacable enemy of humanity, preserving himself by every means, conspires with Nature in her design, which requires the existence of all things. And the descendants of Cain and Abel, although they copy their primitive relatives and perpetually slay each other, live and multiply.

Just listen to what I am about to tell you. Early this morning I went with Teresa and her little sister to the home of an acquaintance of theirs who is on holiday. I was thinking that I would eat in their company, but to my misfortune I had promised the doctor a week ago that I would take lunch with him. If Teresa had not reminded me of it, I would indeed have forgotten.

So I set out almost an hour before midday, but halfway there, overcome by the heat, I lay down under an olive tree. Yesterday's unseasonable wind had been succeeded by a very troublesome heat, and there I was in the shade, without a thought in my head, as though I had already eaten. When I turned my head I was aware of a peasant looking at me, who said brusquely, 'What are you doing here?'

'As you can see, I am resting.'

'Have you any possessions?' striking the earth with the butt of his shotgun.

'Why?'

'Why? Stretch yourself out on your own meadows, if you have any, and don't come trampling other people's grass.'

Then, as he left, 'Just let me catch you here when I come back!'

I had not moved, and he went away. At the very first I had taken no notice of his bravado, but thinking about it again: *If you have any!* If fate had not granted to my forebears a few yards of land, you would have denied me even the last corporal work of mercy – a tomb in the most barren part of your meadow! But, seeing that the olive tree's shadow was stretching out longer, I remembered the lunch.

A short time ago, when I arrived home, I found by my door the same man I had seen in the morning. 'I have been waiting for you, sir. If I have annoyed you, I ask your pardon.'

'Put your hat back on, I was not offended by it.'

Now why is it that on such occasions my heart is sometimes so peaceful and sometimes so stormy?

A certain traveller has said, *'The ebb and flow of my moods governs all my life.'* One minute before perhaps, my indignation would have been much greater than the insult.

Why submit ourselves to the mercy of him who offends us, allowing him to upset us with an unmerited affront? You see how sycophantic self-love tries with this pompous remark to ascribe to my merit an action which comes perhaps from – who knows what? On similar occasions I have not been so reasonable. It is true that half an hour later I have argued against myself, but my reasons were lame, and repentance, for anyone who aspires to wisdom, always comes late. But I don't aspire to it: I am just one of the many sons of this earth, and I carry with me all the passions and the miseries of my kind.

The peasant kept on saying, 'I have been rude to you, but I didn't know who you were. Those workers haymaking in the nearby fields warned me about it afterwards.'

'It doesn't matter, my good chap. What will the harvest be like this year?'

'Poor, and prices will rise. Please, sir, pardon me. I wish to God I had known you!'

'My good man, whether you know someone or not, do not give offence, because you risk either alienating the rich or maltreating the poor. So far as I am concerned, it is not important.'

'You have said well, and God will reward you for it.' And he went away. He may do worse things. He looks rather impudent; and reason in reasonable beings, when they feel no shame, is harmful to anyone who has to deal with them.

Meanwhile? Every day there is a growing number of victims persecuted by the latest usurper of my homeland. How many there may be afflicted, in flight, or in exile, without a bed of sparse grass or the shade of an olive tree, God only knows! The unhappy stranger is even driven from the crags where flocks graze peacefully.

I did not dare, no, I did not dare. I could have embraced her and pressed her to my heart. I saw her asleep. Sleep had closed those large dark eyes, but the roses looked more fresh than ever on her dewy cheeks. Her beautiful body lay relaxed upon a sofa. On one arm she rested her head, and the other hung down listlessly. I have seen her many times walking and dancing. Deep within me I have heard her harp and her voice. I have adored her, full of awe as though I had seen her descend from paradise – but I have never seen her as beautiful as today. Her clothes revealed the contours of that angelic figure; my soul was contemplating it and… what can I say? All the frenzy and ecstasy of love inflamed me and put me beside myself. Piously I touched her clothes and her fragrant hair and the posy of violets which she wore on her breast – yes, yes, beneath this hand, which was so blessed, I felt the beating of her heart. I breathed in the breath from her half-closed mouth. I was about to draw in all the pleasure of those heavenly lips – one kiss, and I would have blessed the tears which I have shed for her so long! – but then, but then I heard her sigh in her sleep. I stepped back, as though impelled by a divine hand. Could it be that I have taught you to love, and to weep? And are you trying to snatch some sleep because I have disturbed your innocent and peaceful nights? At this thought, I fell down prostrate before her and, without moving, held my breath – and then I fled so as not to reawaken her to the distresses of her life. She does not complain, and this torments me all the more; but that face which grows sadder and sadder, and those looks full of pity for me, and that silence at the mention of Odoardo's name, and that sighing for her mother – ah, heaven would not have sent her to us if heaven had not intended her to share our feelings of grief. God Everlasting! Do you exist for us mortals? Or are you an unnatural father to your children? I know that when you sent Virtue, your eldest daughter, into this world, you gave her Misfortune for a guide. But why did you leave Youth and Beauty so weak that they could not bear the discipline of such a stern teacher? In all my afflictions I have raised my arms to you, but I have never dared to murmur or weep. Yet now… Why make me know happiness if I have to desire it so fervently and lose the hope of it for ever? For ever! No, Teresa is all mine. You gave her to me, because you created in me a heart capable of loving her boundlessly, eternally.

If only I were a painter! What rich material there would be for my brush! The artist, obsessed by the delightful idea of beauty, lulls to sleep, or at least soothes, all the other passions. But even if I were a painter? In painters and poets I have seen Nature in her beauty, and at times in her simplicity; but I have never seen Nature depicted at her exalted, immense, inimitable best. Homer, Dante, and Shakespeare, three masters, three superhuman intellects, have taken over my mind and inflamed my heart. I have bathed their verses with warm tears, and I have adored their divine shades as if I saw them seated in the highest spheres of the universe, dominating eternity. The originals, too, which I see before me engage all the powers of my soul, and I would not dare, Lorenzo, I would not dare, even if Michelangelo were transfused into me, to draw even the outlines of them. God in heaven! When you look at an evening in spring, are you pleased with your creation? To comfort me you have given me an inexhaustible source of pleasure, which I have often looked upon with indifference. On the peak of the mountain gilded by the gentle rays of the setting sun, I see myself surrounded by a chain of hills on which harvests ripple, and vines tremble, held up in luxuriant festoons by the olives and the elms. The cliffs and the distant mountain ridges rise up one behind the other. Below me the sides of the mountain are broken into barren gorges where the evening shades, which are rising all the time, grow darker. The dark, horrifying depths look like the mouth of an abyss. To the south a wood overhangs and darkens the valley where the flocks graze in the cool shade, and stray goats seem to hover on the slopes. The birds are singing weakly, as if lamenting the parting day, the heifers are lowing, and the wind seems to delight in the murmuring of the leaves. But to the north the hills separate, and an interminable plain opens out before my eyes. In the nearby fields one can distinguish the oxen coming home. The tired farmer follows them, leaning on his staff; and while mothers and wives prepare supper for their weary families, smoke is rising from the still-white distant villas, and from the scattered cottages. The shepherds are milking their herds, and the old woman who was spinning at the entrance to the sheepfold, leaves her work to caress and stroke the bullock and the little lambs bleating round their mothers. Meanwhile the view stretches on and on, and after long lines of trees and fields, it ends at the horizon where everything dwindles and grows indistinct. The sun throws out a few parting rays, as if these were his last goodbyes to Nature, and the clouds redden, and then grow dim, then colourless, then dark. So the plain disappears, and shadows spread over the face of the earth. And I, as though I were in the middle of the ocean, can see nothing in that direction but the sky.

Only yesterday, after more than two hours' ecstatic contemplation of a beautiful May evening, I was walking slowly down the mountain. The world was under the care of night, and I could hear nothing but the song of a country-girl, and could see nothing but the shepherds' fires. All the stars were sparkling, and as I greeted the constellations one by one, something heavenly took hold of my mind, and my heart was lifted up as though aspiring to a much more sublime region than the earth. I found myself on the hillside near to the church. The death knell was sounding, and a foreboding of my end drew my eyes to the cemetery where, in their grassy mounds, the old forefathers of the hamlet sleep. Rest in peace, you bare remains. Matter has returned to matter, nothing is taken away, nothing is added, nothing is lost down here, everything is changed and reproduced. The human lot! He who fears it less is less unhappy than others. Exhausted, I stretched myself out flat on my face in the pine grove, and in that silent darkness all my misfortunes and all my hopes unrolled before the eyes of my mind. In whatever direction I might run, panting after happiness, I could see, after a hard journey full of mistakes and torment, the grave gaping for me, where I would lose myself and all the ills and all the blessings of this vain life. And I lost heart and I wept, in need of consolation – and in my sobs I called out for Teresa.

14TH MAY

Yesterday evening too, on my way down the mountain, I was tired and I rested beneath those pines. Yesterday evening too I called out for Teresa. I heard footsteps among the trees, and I thought I heard voices whispering. Then I thought I saw Teresa with her sister. At first they were alarmed and fled away. I called them by name, and Isabella

55

recognised me and threw herself on me with a thousand kisses. I arose. Teresa took my arm, and we walked in silence along the bank of the stream as far as Five Springs Lake. And there, as if by agreement, we stopped to gaze at the planet Venus which was shining so brightly. 'Oh!' she said, with her customary, gentle enthusiasm, 'Petrarch must also have come to these lonely places, sighing for his lost love among the peaceful shades of night, don't you think? When I read his poems I picture him here – melancholy, wandering, leaning against the trunk of a tree, feeding upon his own sad thoughts, and looking up to the sky, his tearful eyes searching for Laura's immortal beauty.' I know not how that poor soul, with its heavenly spirit, has been able to survive through so much grief, and continue to dwell among mortal miseries – oh, when one is really in love! And it seemed to me she clasped my hand, and I felt my heart was being torn from my breast. Yes, you were created for me, born for me, and I… I don't know how I managed to stifle these words as they burst from my lips.

She climbed the hill and I followed her. Though my every faculty was enthralled by Teresa, the storm that had aroused such feelings had now subsided. 'Everything is love,' I said. 'The universe is nothing but love! And who has ever felt it more strongly, who has ever made us feel it more sweetly, than Petrarch? Those few geniuses who have raised themselves above so many other mortals fill me with such wonder that they frighten me. But Petrarch fills me with religious confidence and love, and while my intellect sacrifices to him as to a godhead, my heart calls out to him as a father and a comforting friend.' Teresa sighed, yet smiled at the same time.

The climb had tired her. 'Let us rest,' she said. The grass was wet, and I pointed out to her a mulberry tree not far away. The most beautiful mulberry ever. It was high, solitary, leafy. In its branches there was a goldfinch's nest. Ah, how I would love to raise an altar in the shade of that mulberry tree! Meanwhile the little girl had left us, leaping here and there, gathering little flowers and throwing them behind her at the fireflies which came fluttering by. Teresa sat beneath the mulberry tree, and I sat near to her with my head resting on the trunk, reciting Sappho's odes. The moon was rising – oh, why does my heart beat so loudly as I write this? What a blessed evening!

Yes, Lorenzo! I had thought of keeping quiet to you about it – but now you must hear it – my mouth is all dewy – with a kiss from her – and my cheeks have been bathed in Teresa's tears. She loves me – leave me, Lorenzo, leave me in all the ecstasy of this paradisal day.

14TH MAY, IN THE EVENING

Oh, how many times have I taken up my pen once more, and not been able to continue. I feel rather calmer and I am starting to write to you again. Teresa was lying under the mulberry tree – but what can I say that is not all contained in three words? *I love you.* At these words everything I saw seemed like a smile of the universe. I gazed at the sky with my eyes full of gratitude, and it seemed to me that the sky opened to receive us. Alas! Why did death not come then? And I have called on death. Yes, I have kissed Teresa. In that instant the flowers and plants gave out a sweet fragrance. The air was all in harmony. The streams echoed in the distance, and all things were beautified by the splendour of the moon, full as it was of the infinite light that comes from the Divinity. All elements and beings exulted in the joy of two hearts intoxicated with love – I kissed her hand and kissed it again – and Teresa embraced me trembling, and transfused her sighs into my mouth, and her heart beat against this breast. Gazing at me with her large languishing eyes, she kissed me, and her moist half-closed lips murmured to mine – ah, suddenly she pulled away from my breast, as though she were terrified. She called to her sister and ran to meet her. I threw myself down and stretched my arms out as though to take hold of her clothes – but I didn't dare to hold her back or to call her. Her virtue – and not so much her virtue as her passion – left me in dismay. I felt, and I still feel, remorse at having roused that passion in her innocent heart – and it is remorse… remorse at my betrayal! Oh, my cowardly heart! And I approached her trembling. 'I can never be yours!' She spoke those words from the bottom of her heart and with a glance which seemed to reprove herself and pity me. As I went with her along the way, she did not look at me again, and I had no heart to say a word to her. When we reached the garden gate, she took Isabella from my hand and said as she went away, 'Farewell.' And again, turning round after she had taken a few steps, 'Farewell.'

She left me speechless. I could have kissed the prints of her feet. One of her arms was at her side, and her hair, shining in the rays of the moon, was fluttering gently. Then, what with the length of the drive and the dark shadow of the trees, I was just able to see her clothes still blowing white in the distance. And when I lost sight of her, I pricked up my ears to listen for the sound of her voice. And as I went I turned – with my arms opened wide, as if to give myself some comfort – to the planet Venus. But Venus too had disappeared.

15TH MAY

After that kiss I feel divine. My thoughts are more elevated and cheerful, I look more light-hearted, and my heart is more compassionate. Everything seems to grow beautiful at my glance. The plaintive song of birds, and the whisper of the zephyrs among the leaves, are today sweeter than ever. The plants pullulate and the flowers blush beneath my feet. I no longer flee from other men, and it seems that the whole of Nature is mine. Beauty and harmony fill my mind. If I were to sculpt or paint Beauty, I would disdain all earthly models and use only my imagination. O Love! The fine arts are your daughters. You were the first guide upon this earth of sacred poetry, the only nourishment of those generous minds which from their solitude hand down their superhuman songs even to the utmost generations, inciting them with their heaven-inspired words and thoughts to the most noble enterprises. You rekindle in our breasts the only virtue good for mortals – Compassion, which can put a smile upon the lips of the wretch who is condemned to sighs – and it is you, Love, who always revive in living beings that productive pleasure without which all would be chaos and death. If you were to flee away, the earth would become utterly uncongenial: the animals, enemies to each other; the sun, a maleficent fire; and the world, weeping, terror, and universal destruction. Now that my soul is shining in your light, I forget my misfortunes. I laugh at fortune's threats, and renounce the allurements of the future. Oh, Lorenzo! I often lie stretched out on the bank of Five Springs Lake. I feel my face and hair caressed by the breezes which stir the grasses with their breath, and make the flowers rejoice, and cause ripples on the clear waters of the lake. Would you believe it? In my delightful delirium I see before me the naked nymphs, skipping and garlanded with roses, and in their company I call upon the Muses and Love. And out of the sounding, foaming streams I see arising, with their breasts above the water, with their dripping locks falling to their dewy shoulders, and their eyes laughing, the Naiads, the lovable custodians of fountains. '*Illusions!*' cries the philosopher. But is not everything an illusion? Everything! Blessed were the ancients who thought themselves worthy to be kissed by the immortal goddesses of heaven, who sacrificed to Beauty and the Graces, who shed the splendour of divinity on man's imperfections, and who found the Beautiful and the True by cherishing the idols of their fantasy! *Illusions!* But without them I would not feel alive except when I was suffering, or (something which frightens me even more) in harsh and tedious indolence. And when this heart does not wish to feel any more, I shall tear it from my breast with my own hands, and thrust it away like an unfaithful servant.

21ST MAY

Oh, what long painful nights! I am wakened by the fear of not seeing her again. Consumed by a deep, burning, restless presentiment, I leap out of bed and run to the balcony, and do not let my benumbed, naked limbs rest until I see the daylight beginning to dawn in the east. Trembling, I run to her side and, foolishly, I stifle my words and sighs. I cannot think, I cannot hear. Time flies, and night tears me away from that brief paradise. Oh, lightning! You break through the shadows, shine out, cease, and augment the terror and the gloom!

25TH MAY

I thank you, eternal God, I thank you! So you have taken back the spirit which you gave, and Lauretta has left her unhappiness on earth. You hear the groans which come from the depths of the soul, and you send death to free your persecuted and afflicted creatures from the chains of life. My dear friend! At least may your tomb drink in these tears, the only obsequies which I can offer you. May the soil which hides you be protected by fresh grass, and by your mother's blessings and mine. While you lived, you hoped for some comfort from me, and yet I could not even be with you when you were given the last rites. But… we shall meet again, I am sure!

When, my dear Lorenzo, I thought about that poor innocent, I heard a foreboding cry in my soul: *She is dead.* If you had not written to me about it, I would certainly never have known it. Who cares for virtue when it is shrouded in poverty? I have often meant to write to her. The pen fell from my hand, and I bathed the paper with my tears. I was afraid that she would tell me of more suffering, and touch in my heart a chord which would not cease to vibrate for long after. It is only too true that we avoid hearing of the misfortunes of our friends. Their miseries are burdensome to us, and our pride scorns to offer them the comfort of words, so welcome to unfortunate people, when we cannot send with those words some true and real help. It may be that she and her mother numbered me among the crowd of those who, intoxicated with prosperity, forsake the unfortunate. Heaven only knows! Yet God realised that she could not bear any more. *He tempers the wind to the shorn lamb* – shorn indeed, and to the very skin! And you must also remember how one day she came home carrying, closed in her work-basket, a skull – and she lifted the cover, and laughed – and she showed us the skull in the midst of a cloud of roses. *'And there are so many of them,'* she said to us, *'so many of these roses. And I have removed all their thorns. And tomorrow they will wither. But I shall buy others, because every day, every month roses grow and death lays his hand on all of them.'* *'But what do you want to do with them, Lauretta?'* I asked. *'I want to crown this skull with roses, every day with fresh roses.'* And as she answered she laughed pleasantly. And those words and that laugh and that mad look upon her face and those eyes fixed upon the skull and her pale trembling fingers which were interweaving the roses – all that made you too realise how sometimes the desire for death is both necessary and sweet. And also eloquent, even on the lips of a mad girl.

I shall return, Lorenzo. I must get out. My heart swells and groans as though it no longer wished to be in my breast. On the summit of a mountain I feel somewhat freer. But here in my room it is as if I were buried in the grave.

I have climbed the highest of the mountains. The winds were raging. I could see the oaks waving below my feet. The wood was roaring like a stormy sea, and echoing in the valley. The clouds were resting on the rocky slope. In the awesome majesty of Nature my amazed, bewildered soul forgot its troubles, and for a short time was at peace with itself once more.

I would like to speak to you of important matters. They go through my mind. I think about them, they burden my heart, they crowd it out, they become confused. I don't know which one I should begin with, then all of a sudden they forsake me, and I burst into tears.

I am running like a madman, without knowing where or why. I don't realise it, but my feet are drawing me close to precipices. I dominate the valleys and fields beneath me. Magnificent and unexhausted creation! My glances and my thoughts are lost on the distant horizon. I am climbing, and there I stand – upright – panting – I look down: an abyss! Stricken with horror I lift my eyes and I rush down headlong to the mountain's foot where the valley is more gloomy. A grove of young oaks protects me from the winds and the sun. Two rivulets murmur softly as they meander here and there. The branches whisper, and a nightingale – I rebuked a shepherd who had come to take the little ones from their nest. The tears, the desolation, the death of those feeble innocents was to have earned him a few coppers. So it goes! And now, although I have compensated him for what he hoped to gain from them, and – although he has promised not to disturb them any more – do you believe that he won't return to distress them? And there I rest. Where have you gone, you good times that I used to know? My reason is sick and cannot put its trust in anything but sleep. Woe betide it if it felt all its weaknesses. Poor Lauretta! It is almost, almost as if you were calling me. And soon perhaps I shall come.

Everything, everything that exists for men is only their fantasy. Just now among the rocks death terrified me, and in the shade of that grove I would have been glad to close my eyes in everlasting sleep. We construct reality in our own image. Our desires always multiply as our ideas do. We labour for what in a different garb would bore us, and our passions are in the last analysis only the consequence of our illusions. All that I see around me recalls the sweet dream that I had in my boyhood. Oh, how I used to scour these fields with you, seizing upon this or that young fruit tree, forgetful of the past, interested in nothing but the present, exulting in things that were magnified by my imagination and which an hour later no longer existed, and placing all my hopes in the games at the next festivity. But that dream has disappeared! And who can assure me that I am not dreaming at this instant? You can, my God, you who created the human heart. You alone know how fearful is my sleep. You know that nothing remains for me but tears and death.

So I go on raving! My wishes and my thoughts change, and the more beautiful Nature is, the more I wish to see her dressed in mourning. And truly today it looks as though she has heard my prayer. Last winter I was happy. When Nature was in a dead sleep my soul seemed peaceful – and now?

And yet I take comfort in the hope of being pitied. In the dawn of life I may look in vain for the remainder of my time on earth. It will be taken from me by my passions and my misfortunes. But my tomb will be bathed in your tears and the tears of that heavenly girl. Is anyone ever glad to give up this dear and troubled existence for eternal oblivion? Who ever saw the sun's rays for the last time, said farewell for ever to Nature, abandoned his delights, his hopes, his illusions, his very griefs, without casting one wish, one sigh, one glance behind? Those dear to us who survive us are part of us. Our dying eyes ask for pious drops to be shed for us, we would wish our dead bodies to be held in loving arms, and we look for some fond breast over which we may breathe our last sigh. Even from the tomb the voice of Nature cries, and her groans overcome the silence and obscurity of death.[13]

I go over to my balcony now that the sun's powerful light is fading, and shadows are stealing from the universe those feeble rays that flash on the horizon. And in this dull, melancholy, and silent world I recognise an image of the destruction which consumes all things. Then I turn my eyes on the pine copses which my father planted on that hill by the door of the parish church, and I imagine that I can see, white among the foliage as it moves in the wind, my own tombstone. And I seem to see you, coming with my mother to bless, or at least pardon, the ashes of her unhappy son. And to myself, to comfort myself, I prophesy, 'Perhaps Teresa will come alone at dawn to grieve gently over her ancient memories of me, and to bid me once more farewell. No, death is not sorrowful. If someone should come and lay hands on my tomb and disturb my remains, dragging my ardent passions, my opinions, my crimes from the night in which they have been laid to rest, do not defend me, Lorenzo. In answer say only: *'He was a man, and unhappy.'*

26TH MAY

He is coming, Lorenzo. He is coming back.

He has written from Tuscany where he said he would be for twenty days, and the letter is dated 18th May. Within two weeks at most then!

27TH MAY

But I wonder: is it indeed true that this image of a heavenly angel exists here, in this vile world, among us? And I suspect that I may have fallen in love with a creature of my imagination.

And who would not wish to love her, even though unhappily? And where is that man so happy that I would condescend to change for his my tearful state? But how, on the other hand, can I torment myself so much – Do I not see it? Did I not always see it? – without any hope at all? Perhaps she takes some pride in her beauty and in my anguish? She does not love me, and betrayal is smouldering under her compassion. Yet that heavenly kiss from her which is always on my lips and dominates all my thoughts? And her weeping? Ah, but after that moment she has kept away from me, and she does not dare to look me in the face any more. I, a seducer? When I hear thundering within me that awesome judgement: *I can never be yours*, I pass from frenzy to frenzy, and I meditate crimes of blood. Not you, you innocent virgin, but I, I alone have tried to be treacherous, and I might even have consummated my treachery.

Oh, one more kiss from you, and then abandon me to my dreams and my pleasing delirium. I shall die at your feet, but all yours, and with the knowledge at least that I have left you innocent – but at the same time unhappy! You, if you cannot be my bride, will at least be my companion in the tomb. Ah no! Let all the pain of this fatal love be on my head. May I weep through all eternity, but may heaven grant that you be not unhappy for long on my account! But meanwhile I have lost you, and you yourself flee from me. Ah, if you but loved me as I love you!

And yet, Lorenzo, in such wild doubts, and in such great torment, whenever I ask my reason for advice, it comforts me by saying: *You are not immortal.* Well then, let us suffer, even to the last – I shall leave the inferno of this life. And I am self-sufficient. At this notion, I laugh at fortune, at men, and almost at the omnipotence of God.

28TH MAY

Often I imagine this world in chaos, and heaven, and the sun, and the ocean, and all the spheres in flames, in nothingness. But if only in the midst of this universal ruin I could clasp Teresa once more – only once more in these arms – I would cry out for the destruction of all creation.

29TH MAY, AT DAWN

Sheer illusion! In my dreams when my soul is in paradise, and Teresa is at my side, and I feel myself sighing upon her lips, and – why do I then find within myself a void, a void of the tomb? If only those blessed moments had never come, and never fled away! Tonight I was fumbling for that hand which she had pulled away from my breast, and I seemed to hear her groaning in the distance. But the blankets wet with weeping, my head bathed in sweat, my panting breast, the dense and silent darkness – all, all cried out to me: *Wretch, you are delirious!* Frightened and languishing, I threw myself down flat on my face on the bed, clutching the pillow, beginning to torment and beguile myself once more.

If only you could see me tired, desolate, silent, wandering up and down the mountains looking for Teresa, and fearing to find her – often muttering to myself, calling out to her, begging her, and replying to my own words. Burnt by the sun, I plunge into a thicket and fall asleep or rave – ah, how often I greet her as if I could see her, and I dream I clasp her and kiss her… Then she disappears, and I find my eyes are fixed on the edge of some precipice. Yes! I must end it.

29TH MAY, IN THE EVENING

So I must flee – flee: but where? Believe me, I feel ill. I can scarcely drag this body of mine to the villa to comfort myself by the sight of those eyes, and take another sip of life, perhaps the last. Without her, would I want to live in this hell any longer?

A little while ago I said goodbye to her as I was leaving. She did not reply. I went down the stairs, but I could not leave her garden, and – would you believe it? – the sight of her fills me with awe. Seeing her then coming into the garden with her sister I tried to draw back under a pergola and make my escape. Isabella cried out, 'Heaven help us! Haven't you seen us?' As if struck by lightning I dropped down on a seat. The little girl threw her arms round my neck and embraced me, whispering in my ear, 'Why are you always silent?' I don't know if Teresa saw me. She disappeared down an avenue. Half an hour later she came back to call out to the little girl, who was still on my knees, and I saw her eyes were red with weeping. She did not speak to me, but killed me with a glance which seemed to say: 'You have brought me to this.'

2ND JUNE

That is how everything really seems to be. Ah, I did not know that in me there lurked this rage which attacks me, burns me, destroys me, and yet does not kill me. Where is Nature? Where is her immense beauty? Where is the picturesque arrangement of hills which I contemplated from the plain, raising myself in my imagination into the regions of heaven? They look now like naked rocks, and I see nothing but precipices. Their slopes, covered with friendly shade, have become a vexation to me. I walked there once, engaged in the deceptive meditation of our feeble philosophising. What is the use of such meditation if it helps us to know our weakness, but offers no remedy for it?

Today I heard the forest groaning under the blows of axes. The peasants were felling two-hundred-year-old oaks. There is nothing down here that does not perish.

I look at the plants which once I avoided trampling down, and I stop and tear them out of the ground, and I pull off their petals and drop them into the dust which the wind bears along. May the universe suffer with me!

I went out long before the sun was up, and running through the furrows, I tried to stupefy my tempestuous soul with the weariness of my body. My forehead was bathed in sweat, and my breast was panting painfully. The night wind is blowing, disarranging my hair, and chilling the sweat running down my cheeks. Oh, from that time I feel a shudder through all my limbs, my hands are cold, my lips are livid, and my eyes rolling among the clouds of death.

If only her image did not haunt me, wherever I go, standing before me face to face. Because, Lorenzo, she arouses within me a terror, a desperation, an anger, a huge war – and at times I think of seizing her and carrying her away with me into deserts far from the arrogance of men. Oh, how wretched I am! I beat my forehead and I curse. I shall go away.

Perhaps, dear reader, you have become well disposed to Jacopo, and you yearn to know the history of his passion. So, in order to tell you of it, I shall go ahead a little, interrupting the sequence of his letters.

The death of Lauretta exacerbated his melancholy which was made even blacker by the imminent return of Odoardo. He made his visits to the T*** home less frequent, and he did not speak to a single soul. Thin, haggard, his eyes hollow and yet wide open and pensive, his voice deep, his footsteps slow, he usually went about muffled in his cloak, hatless, with his hair falling down over his face. For whole nights he stayed awake, wandering through the countryside, and in the daytime he could often be seen sleeping beneath a tree.

Meanwhile Odoardo came back accompanied by a young painter who was returning from Rome. On the very same day they met Jacopo. Odoardo went to him and embraced him. Jacopo drew back in confusion. The painter said that, having heard tell of him and his intellect, for a long time he had desired to know him personally. Jacopo interrupted him: 'I, sir, have never been able to recognise myself in other people. So I don't believe that other people could ever recognise themselves in me.' *They asked him to explain his ambiguous words. His only answer was to wrap himself up in his cloak and plunge into the trees – and he disappeared. Odoardo complained to Teresa's father of this behaviour. The latter had already begun to be afraid of Jacopo's passion.*

Teresa, endowed with a less morbid sensibility, but passionate and ingenuous, inclined to an affectionate melancholy, deprived in her solitude of all other intimate friendship at the age when we feel the sweet necessity of loving and being loved in return, began to confide in Jacopo, and gradually she fell in love with him. But she did not dare to admit this even to herself, and after the evening of that kiss she became very reserved, avoiding her lover, and trembling in the presence of her father. Far from her mother, with no counsel and no comfort, terrified by the thought of her future state, and by virtue and by love, she became solitary, hardly ever spoke, was always reading, neglected her sketching, and her harp, and her dress, and was often surprised by the family with tears in her eyes. She avoided the company of those young friends of hers who in springtime took *their holidays in the Euganean Hills, and, keeping away from everyone, even from her little sister, she sat for hour after hour in the most secluded parts of her garden. And so in that house there reigned a silence and a certain air of suspicion which troubled her fiancé who was offended also by the scornful behaviour of Jacopo who was incapable of dissimulation. It was natural to him to speak forcefully, and although he was taciturn in conversation, among his friends he was loquacious, always ready to laugh, showing a happiness that was frank, even excessive. But in those days his words and all his actions were as vehement and bitter as his soul. Provoked one evening by Odoardo, who was defending the Treaty of Campoformio, he began to be argumentative, to cry out like someone possessed, to threaten, to beat his own head, and to weep with anger. He had always had an air of authority, but Signor T*** told me that, at that time, he was either lost in thought or, when he was speaking, he would suddenly flare up. His eyes inspired fear, and at times during the conversation he lowered them, bathed in tears. Odoardo became more cautious, and he suspected the reason for the change in Jacopo.*

In this way the whole of June went by. Every day the wretched young man became more gloomy and ill. He did not write to his family any more, and he did not answer my letters. The peasants often saw him riding at full gallop in precipitous places, among thickets, and over ditches, and it was a wonder that he did not come to grief. One morning the painter, who was engaged in depicting the mountains in perspective, heard his voice from somewhere in the wood. He approached stealthily, and heard him declaiming a scene from Saul. *That was when he managed to draw that likeness of Ortis which forms the frontispiece of this edition[14], exactly as he was when he paused in thought after having pronounced these verses from Act 2, scene 1:*

> I would have hurled myself
> Recklessly in among the hostile swords
> A long long time ago; long since cut short
> This dreadful life I am constrained to live.[15]

Then he saw him scramble up to the top of the mountain, look down resolutely with open arms, and all at once draw back exclaiming,

'*O mother!*'

One Sunday he stayed to dinner with the T*** family. He begged Teresa to play, and brought the harp to her himself. As she began, her father came in and sat beside her. Jacopo seemed to be overwhelmed with a pleasurable sadness and looked more and more lively, but gradually he bent his head, and he plunged once more into a melancholy more pitiable than before. Teresa stole glances at him and did her best to hold back her tears. Jacopo noticed this, and not being able to contain himself, he got up and went away. Her father was moved, and turning to Teresa, he said, 'O my child, do you mean to ruin all of us with yourself?' *At these words her tears suddenly gushed forth. She threw herself into her father's arms and confessed everything to him. At this Odoardo entered the room, and Jacopo's sudden departure, Teresa's attitude, and Signor T***'s perturbation confirmed his suspicions. I have heard of all this from Teresa's own lips.*

The following day, which was the morning of 7th July, Jacopo visited Teresa, and he found her fiancé there, and the painter who was painting their wedding portrait. Teresa, confused and trembling, went out hurriedly as though to take care of something she had forgotten, but as she passed in front of Jacopo she said to him anxiously in a whisper: 'My father knows everything.' *He did not say a word or change his expression. He walked up and down the room three or four times, and went out. The whole of that day he did not allow himself to be seen by a living soul. Michele, who was expecting him for dinner, looked for him in vain. He did not return home until past midnight. He lay down on the bed fully clothed, and told the boy to go to bed. A little later he arose and began to write.*

MIDNIGHT

I have been accustomed to give God thanks and to express my wishes to him, but I have never feared him. Yet now that I feel the full force of calamity's whip, I fear him and I supplicate him.

My intellect is blinded, my soul is prostrate, my body is shattered by a deathly languor.

It is true! Those who are unfortunate need another world, not this one where they eat bitter bread and drink water mingled with their tears. The imagination creates another world, and the heart is comforted. Virtue, which is always unhappy down here, perseveres in the hope of some reward, but how wretched are they who need religion in order not to be wicked!

I prostrated myself in a little church in Arquà, because I felt the hand of God was weighing heavily on my heart.

Am I weak, Lorenzo? May heaven never make you feel the necessity of solitude, tears, and a church!

TWO O'CLOCK

The heavens are stormy, the stars are few and pale, and the moon, half buried in cloud, sends its livid rays against my window.

AT DAWN

Can you not hear, Lorenzo? Your friend is calling for you. What a sleep! A ray of light appears, perhaps to impart new vigour to my ills. God does not listen to me. On the contrary, every minute he condemns me to suffer the agony of death, and he makes me curse my days, even though they are not stained with any crime.

What? If you are *a jealous God, visiting the iniquity of the fathers upon the children unto the third and fourth generation,*[16] can I hope to placate you? Send down on me – but not on anyone else but me – your anger which *rekindles the flames of hell* which are to burn millions and millions of people to whom you have not made yourself known. But Teresa is innocent, and far from thinking you are cruel, she adores you serenely. I do not adore you, precisely because I fear you – and I also feel that I need you. Divest yourself, I pray, divest yourself of the attributes with which men have clothed you in order to make you like themselves. Are you not the consoler of the afflicted? And your Divine Son, does he not call himself the *Son of Man*? Hear me, then. This heart feels you, but do not be offended by the groan which Nature wrings from the lacerated heart of man. And I murmur against you, and weep, and call upon you, hoping to liberate my soul. To liberate it? But how, if it is not full of you? If it has not implored you in prosperity, and flies to you for help, and asks you to stretch out your hand, only now when it is prostrate in misery? If it fears you, yet has no hope in you? It hopes for, it desires, only Teresa: and I see you only in her.

There, Lorenzo, from my own lips you have my admission of the crime for which God has withdrawn his countenance from me. I have never adored him as I adore Teresa. Blasphemy! She, equal to God? She, who at a breath will become a skeleton and then nothing? You see man humbled. Ought I therefore to put Teresa before God? Ah, immense heavenly beauty spreads out from her, all-powerful beauty. I measure the universe with one glance. I contemplate eternity with an astonished eye. Everything is chaos, everything vanishes, and everything turns to nothing. God becomes incomprehensible to me, and Teresa is always before me.

Two days later he fell sick. Teresa's father went to visit him, and took the opportunity to persuade him to go far away from the Euganean Hills. Reasonable and fair-minded as he was, he respected Jacopo's mind and spirit, and loved him as the most dear friend that he could ever have. And he assured me that in different circumstances he would have thought it an honour to his family to take for son-in-law a young man who, even if he shared some of the misapprehensions of our time, and was endowed with a stubborn heart, had nevertheless, according to Signor T***, opinions and virtues worthy of ancient times. But Odoardo was rich, and belonged to a family to whose protection Signor T*** was flying from the persecution and snares of his enemies, who accused him of having desired true liberty for his country, a capital crime in Italy. If, on the other hand, he were to ally himself with Ortis by marriage, he would hasten his own ruin and that of his family. Besides which, he had given his word, and in order to keep it he had already gone so far as to separate himself from a wife who was dear to him. Nor did he have the means to marry Teresa off with a large dowry, which would be necessary because of Ortis' modest circumstances. Signor T*** explained all this to me in writing, and he explained it to Jacopo who already knew it, and who listened to him in apparent calm. But as soon as he heard him speak of a dowry, 'No,' *he interrupted him,* 'exiled, poor, unknown to all mankind, I would wish to be buried alive rather than ask you for your daughter's hand in marriage. I am unfortunate, but not therefore base. My children must never owe their good fortune to their mother's riches. Your* daughter is richer than I am, and she is promised to another.' 'Well then?' *replied Signor T***. Jacopo did not breathe a word. He raised his eyes to heaven, and after a long time:* 'O Teresa,' *he exclaimed,* 'you will be unhappy anyway.' 'O my friend,' *said Signor T*** then, in a friendly way,* 'and who began to make her wretched, if not you? She was already, through her love of me, resigned to her state, and she alone was capable eventually of reconciling her poor parents. He has loved her, and you who love her too with such proud high-mindedness, you are taking her fiancé from her, and will foment discord in a house where you were, and are, and will be always received as a son. Give in. Go away for some months. You could have found a sterner father. But I, I too have been unfortunate. I have had feelings, sad to say! And I still have them – and I have learned to sympathise with them, because I too feel the need for sympathy. However, from you alone, at an age when my hair is turning white, I have learned how sometimes we can respect the man who injures us, especially if he is endowed with such a character as to make the affections, which in others are both culpable and risible, seem generous and great. I will not dissemble: from the day when I first made your acquaintance, you have assumed such an inexplicable sway over me that I must both fear and love you. I have often found myself counting the minutes until I would see you again, and I have begun to shudder unexpectedly when the servants told me you were climbing the stairs. Now have pity on me, and on your youth, and on Teresa's reputation. Her beauty and her health are fading. Her heart is being consumed in silence, and for you. I implore you in Teresa's name to take your leave. Sacrifice your passion to her tranquillity, and do not make me at once the most wretched friend, husband, and father that was ever born.' *Jacopo seemed moved. However, his expression did not change, no tear fell from his eye, and he did not answer a word, even though Signor T***, in the middle of his speech, had found it hard to restrain his tears. And he stayed at Jacopo's bedside until the night was far advanced, but neither of them opened his mouth again, except when they bade each other goodnight. The young man's sickness grew worse, and in the following days he was overcome by a dangerous fever.*

Meanwhile, appalled by Jacopo's recent letters, and by those of Teresa's father, I was studying all ways to hasten my friend's departure, the only remedy for his violent passion. I did not have the heart to reveal it to his mother, who had already had many other grievous proofs of his character, and how it was so given to excess. And I merely told her that he was somewhat ill, and that the change of air would certainly help him.

That was the very time when the persecution in Venice began to grow more fierce. There were no laws, but arbitrary tribunals. There were no accusers and no defenders, but rather those who spied on thoughts, new crimes which were unknown to him who was punished for them, and sudden penalties against which there was no appeal. Those who were most suspect languished in gaol; the others, however longstanding and exemplary their reputation, were taken from their homes by night, manhandled by ruffians, dragged to the border and abandoned to their fate, without saying goodbye to their relatives, and destitute of all human aid. For some, exile without this violent and infamous treatment was the greatest mercy they could expect. I too, a tardy martyr but not the last, and not a silent one, have been going for several months as a fugitive through Italy, turning my tearful eyes without any hope at all towards my home. Anxious also for Jacopo's liberty, I persuaded his mother, although she was most distressed, to suggest to him that he should seek refuge in another country until things improved, all the more since when he left Padua he gave these very reasons as his excuse. The letter was entrusted to a servant who arrived in the Euganean Hills on 15th July, and found Jacopo still in bed, but much better. Teresa's father was sitting with him. He read the letter quietly, and put it on his pillow. A little later he read it again, and seemed moved, but he did not speak of it.

On 19th July he left his bed. That very day his mother wrote to him again, sending him money, two bills of exchange, and several letters of recommendation, and imploring him, in the name of God, to depart. Long before evening he went to see Teresa. He found no one but Isabella, who was very touched, and told how he sat in silence, arose, kissed her, and went away. An hour later he returned, and as he was climbing the steps he met her again, and clasped her to his breast, kissed her several times, and bathed her in tears. He settled down to write, kept starting fresh sheets of paper, and then tore them all up. He wandered about sunk in thought in the kitchen garden. A servant, passing by as it grew dark, saw him lying stretched out. Passing by again, the servant found him *standing near the rake, about to go out and with his head turned attentively towards the house which was lit up by the moon.*

When he returned home, he told the messenger to take a reply back to his mother that he would leave at daybreak. He arranged for horses to be ordered at the nearest post. Before going to bed, he wrote the following letter to Teresa, and he delivered it to the gardener. At dawn he departed.

NINE O'CLOCK

Forgive me, Teresa. I have distressed your youth and the peace of your home, but I shall flee. I did not believe I had so much steadfastness. I can leave you, and not die of grief, and that is no small thing. So let us take advantage of this moment, while my heart guides me, and reason does not abandon me quite. True, my mind is preoccupied with the one thought of loving you always and weeping for you. But it will be my duty to write to you no more, and never see you again except when I am certain of leaving you truly at peace. Today I looked for you in vain in order to say goodbye. O Teresa, at least receive these last lines which are bathed, as you can see, in most bitter tears. Send me, at any time and anywhere, your portrait. If friendship, if love, or compassion and gratitude still speak to you in favour of this comfortless man, do not deny me that solace which will sweeten all my sufferings. Your father himself will concede me that, I hope. He will be able to see you, hear you, and feel himself comforted by you. While I, in the eccentricity of my griefs and passions, tired with the whole world, mistrustful of everyone, walking the earth as if from inn to inn, and glad to direct my steps towards the tomb – because I feel very deeply the need of rest – I meantime shall comfort myself by kissing your image day and night. And so from a distance you will inspire me with the constancy to endure this life, and while I have the strength, I will endure it for your sake, I swear. And you, Teresa, I beg you to beseech heaven from the depths of your pure heart – not that I may be spared my griefs, which perhaps I have merited and which are perhaps inseparable from the temper of my soul – but rather that I do not lose those few faculties which I still have, and which enable me to endure my griefs. With your image I shall find my nights less painful, and my solitary days less sad, days through which I shall have to live without you. Dying, I shall turn my last glances to you. I shall commend my last sigh to you. I shall pour out my soul to you. I shall take you with me to the tomb, clasped to my breast. And even if it is ordained that I close my eyes in some foreign land, where there is no one to mourn for me, I shall call you to my deathbed, and I shall imagine I see you in that same attitude, with that same sympathy you had when I saw you once, long before you were able to love me, long before you were aware of my love, and when I was still innocent with regard to you, when you were present during my illness. From you I have only the one letter which you wrote when I was in Padua. That was a happy time, but who would ever have thought so? It seemed to me then that you were urging me to return. And now? Now I am writing the decree, and in a few hours I shall carry out the decree of our eternal separation. From that letter of yours the history of our love begins, and it will never leave me. O Teresa! These are ravings, but they are also the only consolation for one who is incurably unhappy. Farewell. Forgive me, my Teresa. Alas, I thought I was stronger than this. I am writing badly and my words are scarcely legible, but my soul is wounded, and my eyes are weeping. Please do not deny me your portrait. Entrust it to Lorenzo, and if he cannot get it to me, he will keep it as a sacred legacy which will always remind him of your virtues, and your beauty, and the one, eternal, unhappy love of his wretched friend. Farewell! But that is not my last farewell. You will see me again, and from that day onwards I shall be such as to make men have pity and respect for our passion. And for you it will no longer be a crime to love me. Even if, before I see you again, my grief has dug my grave, permit me to make my death dear to me with the certainty that you have loved me. Oh, I do realise in what grief I leave you! Could I only die at your feet: yes, die and be buried in the earth which will receive your bones! But, farewell.

Michele told me that his master travelled for two stages in silence, and with a countenance that was calm, almost serene. Then he asked for his travelling writing-case, and as the horses were being changed again, he started to write the following message to Signor T***.

Dear Sir and friend,

Yesterday evening I gave the gardener a letter to pass on to your daughter. And, although I wrote it when I was already firmly determined to go away, I do fear that I poured onto that paper such affliction as to sadden that innocent lady. Please, sir, be so kind as to make the gardener give you that letter, and I ask you to say to him that he should entrust that letter to no one but you. Keep it sealed or burn it. But because your daughter would be upset if I left her without saying goodbye, and all yesterday I did not manage to see her, I have enclosed here a sealed note. I dare to hope, sir, that you will give it to Teresa T*** before she becomes the wife of the Marquis Odoardo. I do not know if we shall see each other again. But if I have to die, at least I shall die near my father's house. Anyway, if I am disappointed even in this, I am certain, sir, that you will never forget your friend.

*Signor T*** sent the letter for Teresa (which I have included above) to me with its seal unbroken, and he did not delay giving his daughter the note. I have seen it, it was only a few lines, and written by a man who seemed at that moment to have come to himself again.*

Almost all the fragments which follow came to me through the post on different sheets.

ROVIGO, 20TH JULY

I used to gaze at her and say to myself, 'What would become of me if I could not see her any more?' And I ran away to weep by myself, with the consolation of knowing that I was near to her. But now?

What is the nature of the universe now? In what corner of the earth could I live without Teresa? And I dream that I am far from her. Was I so steadfast? And did I have the heart to part thus – without seeing her, without a kiss, without one farewell? Every moment I seem to see her at the door of her house, and I read in her sad face that she loves me. I am fleeing, and at such a speed that every minute takes me further and further from her. And meanwhile? How many fond illusions I have! But I have lost her. I no longer obey my will, my reason, or my bewildered heart. I submit to being dragged along by the sheer force of my destiny. Farewell.

I crossed the Po, marvelling at the immensity of its waters, and more than once I was on the point of throwing myself in, and sinking, and being lost for ever. All at once! Ah, if I had not had a dear, unfortunate mother to whom my death would have been a matter for such bitter tears!

I shall not end my life in such a cowardly manner. I shall bear all my misfortune. I shall weep the last tear that heaven wants me to weep – and when my defences are in vain, and all my passions desperate, and all my strength consumed, when I have the courage to look death in the face, and reason quietly with him, and taste his bitter cup, and make amends for other people's tears, and despair of drying them – well then…

But while I am saying this, is not everything lost? Nothing remains to me but memories and the certainty that all is lost. Have you ever felt that depth of grief when all our hopes desert us?

Not one kiss? No farewell! Although your tears will follow me into the grave. My health, my fate, my heart, you – even you! In short, you all conspire against me, and I shall obey you all.

SOME TIME IN THE NIGHT…

How could I have had the heart to abandon you? O Teresa, I have, in fact, left you in a worse state than myself. Who will comfort you? You will tremble at the mention of my name, because I was the first and only one, in the dawn of your life, who made you aware of the storms and shadows of misfortune. And you, only a young girl, are not yet strong enough either to endure or to flee from life. And you do not yet know that the dawn and evening of life are all one. And I don't wish to convince you of this! And yet we have no more help at all from men, and there is no consolation to be found within ourselves. There is nothing I can do now but entreat the highest God, entreat him with my groans, and look for some hope beyond this world where everyone persecutes us and abandons us. And if the agonies, and the prayers, and the remorse which I have already suffered were an offering acceptable to God, ah, you would not be so unhappy, and I would bless all my torments. Meanwhile, while I am in such mortal desperation, who knows what state you are in! And I cannot defend you, nor dry your eyes, nor gather your secrets into my breast, nor share your afflictions. I do not know where I can flee, nor in what condition I leave you, nor when I shall be able to see you again.

Oh, you cruel father! Teresa is your flesh and blood. The altar of their marriage has been profaned. Nature and heaven curse those vows. Repugnance, jealousy, discord, and repentance will surround that bed and shudder, and stain those chains with blood. Teresa is your daughter: calm down. You will repent this bitterly, but too late. One day, horrified by her condition, she may well curse her days and her parents, and her complaints will disturb your bones, when you will not be able to do anything but listen to her from the grave. Calm down. Alas, you do not hear me. And what are you doing to me? The victim is sacrificed! I can hear her groans, and hear my name in her last groan! Barbarians! Tremble – your blood, my blood – Teresa will be avenged. Ah, delirium! But I too am a killer.

But you, Lorenzo, why do you not help me? I have not written to you because an everlasting tempest of anger, jealousy, revenge, and love was raging within me; and such great passion was swelling in my breast, and stifling me, and almost choking me. I could not breathe a word, and I felt the pain had turned to stone within me, and this pain still prevails, and cuts off my voice and my sighs, and dries up my tears. I feel that most of my vitality has gone, and that little which still remains to me loses heart in the languor and darkness of death.

I am often angry with myself for going away, and accuse myself of cowardice. Why did they not dare to insult my passion? If someone had commanded that unhappy girl not to see me again, if they had torn her from me by force, do you think that I would ever have left her? But is it right for me to reward with ingratitude a father who called me friend, who was often moved to embrace me and say, *'And why has fate brought you to us who are so ill-starred?'* Could I dishonour and bring persecution down on a family who in other circumstances would have shared both my prosperity and my misfortunes? There was no answer I could give him when he sighed and said to me in supplication, *'Teresa is my daughter!'* All my days will be consumed in remorse and solitude.

But I shall always be grateful to that great invisible hand which snatched me away from the precipice where I would have dragged that innocent young girl with me into the abyss. And she followed me. And I, cruel as I was, went away and yet kept stopping and turning my head to see if she was hurrying in my headlong footsteps. And she followed me. But she was frightened, and she had little strength. Am I therefore a seducer? And should I not tear myself away for ever from her sight? Could I only hide myself away from the whole universe and weep over my misfortunes! But how could I weep over the wrongs of that heavenly creature, when I have made them worse?

No one knows what secret is buried within me – and this sudden cold sweat – and this drawing back – and the lament which every evening comes from below the ground and calls me – and that corpse… Lorenzo, I may not be a murderer, and yet I know I am stained with human blood.

The day has scarcely dawned, and I am about to go away. For a long time daybreak has found me sleeping the sleep of a sick man. I never get any peace at night. A short while ago I opened my eyes wide, and howled and rolled my eyes round as if I felt the hangman's hand on my neck. When I awake I am full of terror, like those wretches who have soiled their hands with crime. Farewell, farewell. I am going away, further and further away. I shall write to you from Bologna within the day. Thank my mother. Ask her to bless her poor son. If she knew what a bad state I was in! But stay silent on that matter. Do not give her another wound to add to those she already has.

Part Two

Will you give your friend a crumb of comfort? Ask Teresa to give you her portrait, and then entrust it to Michele whom I am sending to you with the command that he must not return without your reply. You must go to the Euganean Hills. That unfortunate young woman may be in need of sympathy. Read these scraps of letters which I tried to write to you in my dreadful delirium. Farewell. If you see Isabella, give her a thousand kisses from me. When no one else remembers me any more, she may sometimes mention the name of her Jacopo. O my dear friend! Plunged into so much grief, distrustful of men, with an ardent soul which still wants to love and be loved, to whom could I open my heart if not to a little girl still uncorrupted by worldly experience and self-interest, and who in her secret sympathy has bathed me so many times in her innocent tears? If one day I were to learn that she no longer mentioned me, I think I should die of grief.

And you, Lorenzo, tell me: will you forsake me? Friendship, that passion dear to youth and the only comfort for the afflicted, grows cold in prosperity. Oh, friendship, friendship! You will not lose me until I am dead and buried. And at times I shall refrain from complaining of my misfortunes, because without them I might not be worthy of you. I would not have a heart capable of loving you. But when I am no longer alive, when you have inherited my cup of tears – oh, do not look for a friend outside yourself.

I think I would feel somewhat better if I could enjoy a long, heavy sleep. Opium does not help. After a brief lethargy filled with visions and pangs I awaken, just as has happened many nights before! Now I have got out of bed to try to write to you, but I haven't the strength to do it. I shall go back to bed. My soul seems to be in the same black, stormy state as Nature. I hear the rain pouring down. And I lie with my eyes wide open. My God! My God!

It was eighteen days ago that Michele went away again to fetch the post, and he still has not returned, and I do not have your letters. Are you leaving me too? For God's sake, write to me at least. I shall wait until Monday, and then I shall set out for Florence. Here I stay indoors all day because I do not wish to find myself uneasy among so many people, and at night I wander through the city like a ghost, and it breaks my heart to see so many poor people lying in the streets and begging for bread. I don't know whether it is their fault or someone else's. I only know that they ask for bread. Today when I was returning from the post I came across two wretches being led to the scaffold. I enquired of those who were crowding round, and I was told that, out of hunger, one of these men had stolen a mule and the other fifty-six lire. O society! If there were no laws protecting those who, in order to enrich themselves with the sweat and tears of their fellow-citizens, drive them into need and crime, would gaols and executioners be so necessary? I am not so mad as to presume to reorganise mankind, but why should they quarrel with me because I am indignant over their miseries and even more over their blindness? I am told that not a week goes by without such butchery, and the people crowd to it as to a religious ceremony. Meanwhile, crime increases as the penalties for it do. No, no, I don't want to breathe any longer this air tainted with the blood of wretches. But where shall I go?

FLORENCE, 27TH AUGUST

Just now I have been adoring the tombs of Galileo, Machiavelli, and Michelangelo, and as I approached them I found myself shuddering. Do those who have erected these mausoleums hope to avoid blame for the poverty and imprisonment with which their ancestors punished the greatness of these divine intellects? Oh, how many of those who are persecuted in our century will be venerated by posterity! But persecution of the living, and honours for the dead, bear witness to the malign ambition which tortures the human herd.

Near these marble monuments I felt myself living again those ardent years of mine when, staying up late over the writings of great men, I imagined myself enjoying the applause of future generations. Such thoughts are too elevated for me now! They may even be mad. My intellect is blind, my limbs unsteady, and my heart corrupt, here, in its very depths.

Keep the letters of recommendation you mentioned in your letter. I have burned those which you sent me. I don't want any more insults, or any favours from influential men. The only mortal whom I wanted to meet was Vittorio Alfieri, but I hear that he refuses to make fresh acquaintances, and I would not presume to ask him to break this resolution of his, which is probably the result of the times in which we live, his studies, and even more his passions and his experience of the world. And even if it were a weakness, the weaknesses of such mortals should be respected. And he who has none, let him cast the first stone.

Open the windows wide, Lorenzo, and from my room greet my hills. On a beautiful September morning greet in my name the sky, the lakes, the plains, all those reminders of my boyhood, places where for some time I rested from life's anxieties. If, on your walks in cloudless nights, your feet were to lead you towards the avenues near the parish church, I beg you to climb up the hill of pines which preserves so many sweet and bitter memories of mine. At the foot of the slope, once you have passed the grove of limes which keeps the air always fresh and perfumed, there where those rivulets meet in a little lake, you will find the solitary willow under whose weeping branches I lay prostrate for many hours thinking of all my hopes. And when you come near the summit you may hear a cuckoo which seemed to call me every evening in its mournful metre, which it only interrupted when it became aware of my muttering and the tread of my feet. The pine in which it used to hide itself casts a shadow over the ruins of a little chapel where in ancient times a lamp used to burn before a crucifix. It was shattered by the storm in that night which has left my spirit even today, and as long as I live, terrified by shadows and remorse. And those half-buried ruins in the darkness looked to me like sepulchral stones, and I often thought of erecting my tomb there among those secret shades. And now? Who knows where I shall leave my bones? Comfort all those peasants who ask for news of me. A long time ago they used to crowd around me, and I called them my friends, and they called me their benefactor. I was the doctor who was most welcome when their little ones were sick. I listened sympathetically to the complaints of those poor workers, and settled their quarrels. I philosophised with those simple people in their feeble old age, racking my brains to drive the terrors of religion out of their minds, and describing the rewards which heaven reserves for the man weary with poverty and hard work. But now they will mention me with sadness, because in these last months I have passed them by, silent and eccentric, sometimes without responding to their greetings. And when I perceived them at a distance singing on their way home from work, or bringing the cattle home, I kept out of their way, hiding myself where the wood is thickest. And they saw me in the dawn leaping the ditches and heedlessly bumping into the saplings, which rained hoar frost down upon my head as they bent over. They saw me rush across the meadows, and then clamber up the highest hill, where I stood panting, with my arms stretched to the east, waiting for the sun so that I could complain to him that he no longer rose happily for me. They will point out to you the edge of the rock where, while the world slept, I sat listening to the distant roar of the waters and the rumblings in the air as the winds massed the clouds above my head, driving them to obscure the setting moon whose pale rays lit up from time to time the crosses on the mounds in the cemetery. And then a peasant in a nearby hovel, wakening in alarm at the sound of my cries, would go to the door, and in that solemn silence listen to me praying, and weeping, and howling, and gazing down at the tombs, and invoking death. O my former solitude! Where are you? There is no stretch of land, no cave, no tree which does not arouse again in my heart that sweet and pathetic desire which always accompanies the unlucky exile far from home. It seems to me that my pleasures and my pains, which in those places were dear to me – everything in fact which is mine – has remained there with you, and that here it is only the ghost of poor Jacopo which is dragging itself along on its pilgrimage.

But you, my only friend, why do you write scarcely two words, merely to tell me that you are with Teresa? And you do not tell me how she lives, nor if she dares to mention me, nor if Odoardo has snatched her away from me. I run to the post again and again, but to no avail, and I come back slowly, bewildered, and in my face there can be read the presentiment of some heavy calamity. And from time to time I seem to hear the sentence which is fatal to me: *Teresa has made her vows.* Alas!

When will there be an end of my funereal frenzies and my cruel illusions? Farewell.

You have driven my heart to desperation. I see now that Teresa is trying to punish me for having loved her. She had sent her portrait to her mother before I asked for it? You assure me of that, and I believe you, but take care lest, in trying to bring me back to health, you deprive me of the one comfort for my wounded heart.

Oh, my hopes! They all leave me, and I sit here abandoned in the solitude of my grief.

In whom can I trust now? Do not betray me, Lorenzo. You will never leave my breast, because your friend has need of your memory. You would not have been without me in any adversity of yours. So I am destined to see myself disappear completely? Even down to the last scrap of hope I have? So be it! I shall not complain of her, or of you, or of myself, or of my fate. I am degrading myself with so much weeping, and forfeiting the consolation of being able to say: '*I endure my troubles and do not lament.*'

You will all leave me, all. And my groans will follow you everywhere, because without you I am not a man. And wherever I am I shall call upon you in my despair. These are the few words which Teresa has written to me: 'Respect your life. I beseech you in the name of our misfortune. We are not the only unhappy ones. You will have my portrait when I am able to send it. My father sympathises with me, and he does not mind that I am replying to the note which he gave me from you. However, his silent tears prohibit me from writing henceforth. And I weep and promise I shall not. And I am writing to you, perhaps for the last time, weeping, because I can no longer admit I love you, except to God alone.'

So you are stronger than I am? Yes. I shall repeat these few lines as if they were your last wishes. I shall speak to you once again, Teresa, but only on that day when reason and courage give me so much strength that I am able really to separate myself from you.

If only loving you with this immense, unendurable love, and remaining silent and burying myself away from everyone's eyes, could give you peace again! If only my death could expiate your passion before the tribunal of our persecutors, and lull it to sleep for ever in your breast – then with all my heart and soul I would beg Nature and heaven to take me from this world at last. Now I promise you that I shall resist my fatal, sweet desire for death. But that I shall overcome it, ah! You alone, by your prayers, may be able to obtain that for me from my Creator; and I sense that he is calling me anyway. But you, I beg you, live as happily as you can, as happily as you still can. God may console you with these penitent tears which I weep as I ask him to pity you. It is only too true that you share my desolate condition, that through me you have been made unhappy. And look how I have rewarded your father for his affectionate care, for his trust, for his advice, for his kindnesses! And you, in what an abyss you have found yourself, and still find yourself, because of me! How has your father benefited me! Should I not today recompense him with silent gratitude? Should I not present him with my bloodstained heart as a sacrifice? No mortal is my creditor in generosity. And I, even though I am, as you well know, a very strict judge of myself, cannot blame myself for having loved you – even though causing you grief is the most cruel crime that I could ever commit.

Alas! To whom am I speaking? And to what purpose?

If this letter finds you when you are still among my hills, Lorenzo, do not show it to Teresa. Do not speak to her about me. If she asks about me, say that I am alive, still alive. In short, do not speak of me. But I confess to you that I am glad of my weaknesses. I finger my wounds where they are most grievous, and I try to ulcerate them, and I look at them as they bleed. And it seems to me that my sufferings are some expiation for my faults, and a brief comfort for the griefs of that innocent young girl.

FLORENCE, 25TH SEPTEMBER

It was in this blessed region that the sacred Muses and humane letters awakened from barbarism. Wherever I turn my eyes, I see the houses where they were born, and the sacred earth where those first great Tuscans rest. At every step I am afraid of trampling on their remains. The whole of Tuscany is one large city, and a garden. The people are kind by nature. The sky is cloudless, and the air full of life and health. But your friend finds no rest. I always hope – tomorrow, in the next town – and tomorrow comes, and here I am wandering from town to town, and I am more and more weighed down by this state of exile and solitude. I am not even allowed to continue on my journey. I had decided to go to Rome to pay homage to the remains of our grandeur. They are denying me a passport. That which my mother sent me is for Milan, and here, as if I had come to plot, they have surrounded me with a thousand questions. Perhaps they are not wrong to do so, but I shall reply tomorrow with my departure. So all we Italians are political exiles and foreigners in Italy, and when we are only a short distance away from our own little bit of earth, neither intellect, nor fame, nor a blameless life protects us. And woe betide you if you dare to show an ounce of true courage! The moment we are exiled from our own doors, we find no one to receive us. Plundered by some, scorned by others, always betrayed by everyone, forsaken even by our fellow-citizens, who instead of sympathising and giving help in the common disaster, regard as barbarians all those Italians who are not from their province, and whose limbs do not rattle with the same chains – tell me, Lorenzo, what refuge is there left for us? Our harvests have enriched our rulers, but our lands provide neither shelter nor bread to so many Italians whom the revolution has driven beyond their native sky, and who, faint through hunger and weariness, hear always whispering in their ears the one ultimate counsellor of the man deprived of all that Nature requires – crime! And so for us what refuge now remains but the desert, and the tomb? And dishonour! And he who dishonours himself most, may live the better for it, but ashamed of himself, and mocked by those very tyrants to whom he sells himself, and by whom one day he will be sold.

I have travelled throughout Tuscany. All its hills and fields are famous for those fraternal battles of four centuries ago. And meanwhile the corpses of an infinite number of slaughtered Italians have formed the foundations for the thrones of the Emperors and the Popes. I climbed to Monteaperto where the memory of the defeat of the Guelphs is still notorious. Day was just dawning, and in that sad silence, and in that cold darkness, with my soul assaulted by all the ancient and cruel misadventures which lacerate our homeland – O my Lorenzo, I felt myself shiver, and the hair rose on my head. I shouted from the height in a voice full of threats and fear. And I imagined I could see the shades of all those Tuscans who had been killed, climbing and descending the steepest slopes of the mountain, their swords and clothes stained with blood, looking sullenly around, and trembling in anger, and coming to blows and reopening ancient wounds. Oh, for whom was that blood shed? The son cuts his father's head off and swings it round by the hair. Who benefits from that wicked slaughter? The kings for whom you are slaughtered shake hands in the heat of the battle and peacefully divide your clothes and your land. I fled away, howling and gazing behind me. And those horrible images kept on following me, and when I find myself alone at night, I see those spectres around me still, and with them one spectre more fearful than all, whom I alone know. And why must I always accuse you, my homeland, and sympathise with you, with no hope at all of ever being able to improve you or help you?

MILAN, 27TH OCTOBER

I wrote to you from Parma, and then from Milan the day I got there. A week ago I wrote you a very long letter. So why has your letter turned up so late, and by way of Tuscany from which I have been gone since 28th September? I strongly suspect that our letters are being intercepted. The governments boast that goods are safe, but at the same time they invade privacy, the most precious of all things we have. They prohibit silent complaints, and they profane the sacred refuge which misfortunes look for in friendship's breast. That's how it is! I should have foreseen it. But those scoundrels of theirs will no longer go hunting after our words and our thoughts. I shall pay to make sure that our letters travel unprofaned from now on.

You ask me for news of Giuseppe Parini. He has not lost his nobility and pride, but I think he is daunted by the times and by old age. When I went to visit him, I met him at the door of his apartments as he was dragging himself out. He recognised me and, leaning on his stick, he put his hand on my shoulder, saying, 'You have come again to see this spirited horse which, in its heart, still feels the pride of its glorious youth, but which now slumps along the way, and rises again only at fortune's blows.'

He is afraid of being expelled from his professorship and finding himself constrained, after seventy years of studies and glory, to die begging for his bread.

MILAN, 11TH NOVEMBER

I asked a bookseller for the autobiography of Benvenuto Cellini. They do not have it. I asked for another writer, but he said, rather spitefully, that he did not sell Italian books. The civilian population speaks an elegant French, and pure Tuscan is scarcely understood. Public documents and the laws are written in such a bastard language that the bare phrases bear witness to the ignorance and servitude of those who dictate them. In the Cisalpine Republic our followers of Demosthenes have had heated debates in their senate to exile the Greek and Latin languages upon pain of death. One law has been passed whose only purpose was to deprive the mathematician Gregorio Fontana and the poet Vincenzo Monti of all employment. I don't know what they may have written against Liberty, before Liberty lowered herself into prostitution in Italy. I do know that they are also ready to write for her. And whatever their fault may have been, the injustice of their punishment absolves them from it, and the formality of a law enacted just for two individuals increases their celebrity. I asked where the Legislative Councils met. Few understood me, fewer still replied, and no one could tell me.

MILAN, 4TH DECEMBER

Let this be my only reply to your counsels. In all countries I have found men to be of three kinds: the few who command, the majority who serve, and the many who intrigue. We cannot command, and perhaps we are not cunning enough for that. We are not blind, and we do not wish to serve. We do not descend to intrigue. And the best course is to live like those masterless dogs which receive neither stale crusts nor blows. Why do you want me to cadge protection and employment in a state where I am reputed a foreigner, and from which I could be exiled at the whim of any spy? You who are always extolling my intellect, do you know what I am worth? Neither more nor less than my income. That is, if I do not become a *courtly man of letters*, curbing that noble audacity which vexes the powerful, and concealing my virtue and knowledge, so that they do not feel reproved for their ignorance and villainy. Men of letters indeed! But you will say that things are like this everywhere. So be it. I let the world go its own way, but if I had to meddle with it, I should want men either to change their ways or command my head to be struck off on the scaffold. And the latter seems the more likely. It is not that the petty tyrants are unaware of the intrigues, but men who have gone in one bound from the streets to the throne have need of fanatics, whom they cannot then control. Arrogant in the present, careless of the future, poor in fame, courage, and intellect, they arm themselves with flatterers and satellites, from whom, although they are often betrayed and scorned, they are no longer able to break free: a perpetual cycle of servitude, licence, and tyranny. In order to become master and thief of the people's goods, a man must first let himself be oppressed and despoiled, and must lick the sword that drips with his own blood. In this way I might be able to get myself a post, some thousands of *scudi* more per year, remorse, and infamy. Let me say it once more: *I shall never play the part of the petty villain.*

I know I have been trampled on very many times, but only as one of an immense crowd of fellow-slaves, like those insects which are heedlessly squashed by passers-by. Unlike so many others, I do not glory in my servitude, nor do my tyrants feed on my humiliation. Let them keep for others their insults and their benefits. There are still many left who yearn for them! I shall flee from shame by dying unknown. And if I were forced to come out of my obscurity, well then, rather than show myself to be a successful instrument of licence and tyranny, I would choose to be a lamented victim.

If I lacked for bread and warmth, and if what you point out to me were the only source of life (heaven forbid that I should insult the necessity of all those others who could not follow my lead), truly, Lorenzo, I should go away to our common fatherland, where there are no informers, or conquerors, or courtly men of letters, or princes, where crime is not rewarded with riches, where the poor man is not executed simply because he is a poor man, where sooner or later everyone will come to dwell with me and be mingled with matter, beneath the ground.

Clinging to the precipice of life, I follow from time to time a lamp which I perceive in the distance and which I can never reach. Indeed, I think that if my whole body were in the grave, and only my head remained above ground, I should always see that lamp flashing on my eyes. O Glory! You always run before me, luring me on a journey on which my feet cannot bear me. But from the day when you ceased to be my one and only passion, your radiant phantom has begun to fade away and reel and stagger. It falls, and it becomes a heap of bones and ashes which I see from time to time giving out some pale rays. Very soon, O Glory, I shall walk over your skeleton, smiling at my disappointed ambition. How often, ashamed of dying unknown in my time, I have myself flattered my anguish, while I felt all the necessity of ending it, and the courage to do so! I might not have survived the death of my homeland if I had not been held back by the foolish fear that the stone placed over me would bury my name with my body. I confess that I have often regarded the misfortunes of Italy with a certain pleasure, since I thought that fate and my own audacity were reserving for me the honour of liberating my country.

Yesterday evening I was telling Parini… Goodbye – the messenger from the bank is here to take this letter, and I have come to the end of this page – a sign that I should finish. However, I have much more to tell you. I shall put off sending my letter until Saturday, and go on writing it now. Here we are, after so many years of affectionate and loyal friendship, separated, and perhaps for ever. My only comfort is in weeping with you as I write to you, and in this way I free myself somewhat from my thoughts, and my solitude becomes much less fearful. You know how many nights I wake up, and get out of bed, and call upon you as I walk slowly round my apartments! I sit down and write to you, and those pages are all stained with tears and filled with my piteous delirium and my ferocious intentions. But I have not the heart to send them to you. Some of them I keep, and many I burn. So when heaven grants me these moments of calm, I write to you with as much strength of mind as I can muster, lest I sadden you with my great grief. I shall not tire of writing to you. All other comforts are lost. Nor will you, my Lorenzo, tire of reading these pages which – without vanity, without study, and without blushing – I have written to you, always in the greatest pleasures and the worst griefs of my soul. Keep them. I have a presentiment that one day you will have need of them in order to live, as much as you can, with your Jacopo.

Well then, yesterday evening I went walking with that venerable old man in the eastern suburbs of the city in a grove of limes.[17] He supported himself on one side on my arm, and on the other with his stick, and occasionally he looked at his crippled feet, and then turned to me without saying a word, as though complaining of his infirmity and thanking me for the patience with which I accompanied him. He sat down on one of those benches and I sat down too. His servant kept a short distance away from us. Parini is the most dignified and eloquent person whom I have ever known. However, to whom does a profound, large-minded, deeply pondered grief not give supreme eloquence? He spoke to me at length of his homeland, and shuddered at the ancient tyrannies and the recent licence. Letters were prostituted, all the passions were degenerate and languishing into vile and indolent corruption, there was no more sacred hospitality, no more benevolence, no more filial love. And then he went over recent events, and the crimes of so many manikins whom I would stoop to name if only their villainies revealed the strength of mind – I shall not say of Sulla or Catiline – but of those spirited robbers who face their wrongdoing squarely, even at the foot of the scaffold. But these are petty, fearful, arrogant thieves. In short it is more honest to stay silent about them. At those words I blazed with superhuman fury, and arose, crying out, 'Why do we not make an effort? Shall we die? But an avenger will spring from our blood.' He looked at me in astonishment. In that uncertain light my eyes flashed in a frightening way, and my humble and pale appearance took on a threatening air. I fell silent, but I still felt a shudder rumbling gloomily within my breast. And I resumed, 'Will there never be any salvation for us? Ah, if men lived always with Death for companion, they would not be such cowardly slaves.' Parini did not open his mouth, but clutching my arm, he looked at me more and more fixedly. Then he pulled me as if indicating that I should sit down again. 'And do you think,' he burst out, 'that if I could see one gleam of liberty,

94

I would give myself over to these vain laments, despite my infirmity and old age? O young man, you are worthy of a more grateful homeland! If you cannot extinguish your fatal ardour, why do you not direct it to other passions?'

Then I looked into the past, and thence I turned eagerly to the future, but I found myself always wandering in a void, and my disappointed arms closed without ever clasping anything, and I realised all the desperation of my state. I told that noble Italian the history of my passion, and I described Teresa as one of those spirits which seem to descend from heaven to illuminate this life's dark room. And at my words and tears the sympathetic old man sighed very often from the depths of his heart. 'No, no,' I said to him, 'I see nothing ahead of me but the grave. I am the son of an affectionate and generous mother. I have often seemed to see her treading in my footsteps and following me to the summit of the mountain from which I was about to cast myself off, and when my body was almost in the air, she seized me by my coat-tails and pulled me back, and as I turned I could hear nothing but her weeping. However, if she knew of all my hidden woes, she would herself beg heaven to put an end to my anxious days. But the only vital flame which still animates this tormented body is my hope of liberty for our homeland.'

Parini smiled sadly, and when he realised that my voice was growing hoarse, and I was gazing fixedly at the ground, he recommenced, 'This rage of yours for glory could lead you into difficult undertakings. But, believe me, heroes owe their fame, one quarter to their boldness, two quarters to fate, and the other quarter to their crimes. Even if you thought yourself lucky enough and wicked enough to aspire to this glory, do you think these times of ours would offer you the means? Have the groans of all the ages and this yoke which now lies upon our homeland still not taught you that one cannot expect liberty from a foreigner? Whoever gets involved in the affairs of a conquered land achieves nothing but public harm and his own infamy. When duties and rights are at the point of a sword, the strong man writes the laws in blood and claims that virtue must be sacrificed. And then? Can you pretend to the fame and valour of Hannibal who, when he was a fugitive, searched the whole universe for an enemy to Rome? Nor will you be allowed to be righteous with impunity. An upright young man, with an ardent heart, but without wealth, and temperamentally incautious, such as you are, will always be a tool of faction, or a victim of the powerful. And if in public affairs you can keep yourself uncorrupted by the general nastiness, oh! you will be highly praised. But then you will be killed by calumny, that dagger in the night. Your prison will be forsaken by your friends, and your tomb scarcely honoured by a single sigh.

'But supposing that you were able to aspire to your goal, overcoming the arrogance of foreigners, the malignity of your fellow-citizens, and the corruption of these times – tell me, will you shed all the blood with which a nascent republic must be nourished? Will you burn your houses in the flames of civil war? Will you unite the parties with terror? Will you extinguish opinions with death? Will you even out men's prosperity with massacres? If you fall by the wayside, you will find yourself cursed by some as a demagogue, by others as a tyrant. The favour of the multitude is short-lived and fatal. They judge by the outcome, rather than by intentions. They think crime is virtuous when it is expedient, and they think integrity is wicked when they fear to lose by it. And to have their applause, one must terrorise them, or fatten them up, or deceive them all the time. So be it. Could you, when you were swollen with pride in your boundless good fortune, repress your lust for supreme power, fomented in you by your feeling of superiority and your knowledge of the common humiliation? Mortals are by nature slaves, by nature tyrants, and by nature blind. Intent on bolstering up your throne, you will change from a philosopher into a tyrant, and for a few years of power and trepidation, you would relinquish your peace of mind and your name would be confused with others' in the immense crowd of despots.

'There still remains the possibility of a place among the captains, one won by ferocity and boldness, by a greed which seizes in order to squander, and by a baseness which licks the hand which helps you to climb. But, my son, humanity groans at the birth of a conqueror, and its only comfort is the hope of smiling on his bier.'

He fell silent. After a long silence I exclaimed, 'O Cocceus Nerva! You at least knew how to die uncontaminated by the corruption you saw coming.' The old man looked at me. 'If you have no hope, and no fear of anything beyond this world –' and he clasped my hand – 'but I…' He raised his eyes to heaven, and his stern face became milder with some sweet comfort, as if he were contemplating all his hopes above. I heard a sound of trampling coming towards us, and then I caught a glimpse of people among the limes. We stood up, and I accompanied him to his apartments.

Ah, if only I did not feel it was now spent within me, that celestial fire which in the time of my first youth illuminated everything around, while today I am groping in vacuity and darkness! If only I had somewhere where I could sleep secure. If only I were not prevented from taking refuge again in the darkness of my hermitage! If only a desperate love which my reason is always fighting against, but can never conquer – this love which I conceal even from myself, but which flares up again every day, and which has become omnipotent, immortal – ah, Nature has endowed us with this passion which is more indomitable than the fatal instinct for life – if only, in short, my prayers could obtain for me a single year of calm, your friend would wish to fulfil one more vow and then die. I hear my homeland crying out to me, *Write what you have seen. I shall send my voice out from the ruins and tell you my story. The centuries will weep over my solitude, and the peoples will be taught by my misfortunes. Time strikes down the strong, and crimes of blood are washed in blood.'* And you know, Lorenzo, that I would have the courage to write, but my mind is dying at the same time as my physical strength, and I see that within a few months I shall have completed my distressful pilgrimage.

But you few sublime intellects, solitary and persecuted, who tremble at the ancient wrongs of our homeland, if heaven prevents you from fighting force with force, why do you not at least tell posterity of our misfortunes? Raise your voices in everyone's name, and say to the world that we may be unfortunate, but are neither blind nor base, that it is not courage which we lack, but power. Even if your arms are in chains, why do you yourselves put fetters on your intellects, over which neither tyrants nor fortune, arbiters of all things, have any control? Write. However, have pity on your fellow-citizens. Do not vainly stir up their political passions, but hold the majority of your contemporaries in contempt. The human race today has the frenzies and the weakness of decrepitude, but the human race, at the very point of death, revives in all its vigour. Write to those who are to come, and who alone will be worthy to hear you, and strong to avenge you. Persecute your persecutors with the truth. And since you cannot oppress them, while they live, with daggers, oppress them at least with opprobrium for all future ages. If some of you have had your homeland, your tranquillity, and your possessions seized, if no one dares to marry, if everyone fears the sweet name of father, not wishing to procreate in exile and grief new slaves and new unfortunates, why are you so base as to cherish a life devoid of all pleasure? Why do you not consecrate your life to the one phantasm which guides magnanimous men – Glory? You will judge Europe as it now is, and your judgement will enlighten people who are still to come. Human baseness displays its terrors and dangers. But are you by any chance immortal? From the humiliation of prisons and tortures you will rise above the man of power, and his fury against you will augment his disgrace and your fame.

MILAN, 6TH FEBRUARY 1799

Address your letters to Nice, because tomorrow I am setting out for France, and perhaps much further. Who knows? I shall certainly not stay long in France. Don't be sorry about that, Lorenzo, and comfort my poor mother as well as you can. You may say that I ought first to flee from myself, and that if there is nowhere where I can be at peace, it is about time that I resigned myself to that. It is true, I do not find any peace, but it is worse here than elsewhere. The season, the perpetual cloud, this dead atmosphere, certain physiognomies, and then – perhaps I deceive myself – but it seems to me I can find little heart. Nor can I blame them: everything can be gained, but compassion and generosity, and even more a certain delicacy of mind, are always born with us, and only he who feels them looks for them. And so I am off tomorrow. And the need to go away is so firmly fixed in my imagination that these hours of delay seem to me like years in prison.

Ill-omened creature! Why is it that all your senses can be aroused only by grief, like those flayed limbs which shrink from the most gentle breath? Enjoy the world as it is, and you will live more peacefully, and less madly. But suppose I were to say to him who preached me such sermons, 'When you are overcome by a fever, make your pulse beat more slowly, and you will be well.' Would he not be right to think that I was raving in the delirium of a worse fever? So how could I lay down the law to my blood, which fluctuates so rapidly? When it crashes into my heart I feel it massing there and seething, and then it gushes out impetuously. And often all of a sudden, and sometimes when I am asleep, it seems as though it is about to split my breast open. O you, as wise as Ulysses! Here I am, ready to obey what your wisdom advises, on one condition: when I see you dissimulating, cold, incapable of succouring poverty without insulting it, or of defending the weak against injustice; when I see you, in order to satisfy your vulgar little passions, prostrate at the feet of the man of power whom you hate and who despises you – then may I be allowed to transfuse into you a drop of this ardent rage of mine. It has often strengthened my voice and my arm against bullying. It never lets my eyes stay dry nor my hand closed at the sight of misery. It will always save me from baseness. You think you are wise, and the world says you are honest. But don't worry. Don't be troubled. Our roles are equal: God preserve you from my *madness*, and with all the strength of my soul I pray him to preserve me from your *wisdom*.

If I catch sight of those people, Lorenzo, even when they are passing by without seeing me, I immediately run to take refuge in your breast. Such is your affection that you respect my passions, although you have often seen the lion grow tame at the mere sound of your voice. But now you see how it is: every counsel and every reason is fatal to me! Woe betide me if I do not obey my heart! Reason? It is like the wind. It blows torches out, and stirs up conflagrations. Meanwhile, farewell.

TEN O'CLOCK IN THE MORNING
On thinking it over, it will be better if you do not write to me until you have my letters. I am taking the road through the Ligurian Alps in order to avoid the ice on Mont-Cenis. You know how harmful the cold is to me.

ONE O'CLOCK

A further obstacle. It will be another two days before I have my passport back. I shall send this letter when I am about to get into the calash.

8TH FEBRUARY, HALF PAST ONE

Here I am weeping over your letters. As I was rearranging my papers I came across these few lines which you wrote to me under a letter from my mother two days before I left my hills: 'All my thoughts go with you, O my Jacopo. My vows go with you, and my friendship, which will live for ever. I shall always be your friend and your loving brother, and I shall even share my soul with you.' Do you know that I go on repeating these words, and I feel myself struck so forcibly by them that I am on the point of coming to throw myself about your neck and breathe my last in your arms? Farewell, farewell. I shall come back.

THREE O'CLOCK

I have been to say goodbye to Parini. 'Farewell, you unfortunate young man,' he said. 'Everywhere and always you will take with you your generous, always unsatisfied passions. You will always be unhappy. There is no consolation in any advice I could give, because my advice does not help me in my misfortunes which come from the same source as yours. Old age has benumbed my limbs, but the heart is still alive. The only comfort I can offer you is my sympathy, and you have it all. In a little while I shall be dead, but if my ashes still have some feeling, or rather, if it is some relief to you to lament over them, then come to my grave.' I burst into a flood of tears, and left him. And he came out, following me with his eyes for the length of that long, long corridor, and I understood what he was saying again and again, his voice full of tears – farewell.

NINE O'CLOCK IN THE EVENING

Everything is arranged. The horses have been ordered for midnight. I am going to lie down, dressed as I am, until they arrive. I am so worn out. In the meantime, farewell, farewell, Lorenzo. I am writing your name and saying a fond goodbye to you with a certain superstitious feeling which I have never ever experienced before. We shall meet again. If only we could! No, I will not die without seeing you again and thanking you for ever – and you, my Teresa! But since my unhappy love would cost you your peace of mind and your family's tears, I am in flight, without knowing where my destiny will drag me off to. The Alps and the ocean, and a whole world if possible, must divide us.

GENOA, 11TH FEBRUARY

How beautiful the sun is here! All the fibres of my being are shaking with pleasure at the joyfulness of this shining, healthy sky. I am glad I came away. And yet I am travelling on in a few hours. I still can't say where I will stop, nor when my journey will finish, but by 16th February I shall be in Toulon.

PIETRA LIGURE, 15TH FEBRUARY

Mountain roads and grim, precipitous steeps, all the severity of the weather, all the weariness and tedium of the journey, and then? *'New torments and new people being tormented.'*[18]

I am writing from a little village at the foot of the Maritime Alps. I have had to stop here for a while because there are no horses at the inn, and I don't know when I shall be able to leave. So here I am, always with you, and always with new afflictions. I am fated not to move one step without coming across grief along the way. These last two days I have been going out towards noon for a mile or so from the built-up area, walking through olive groves near the seashore. I do this because it comforts me to be in the light of the sun, and I like to drink the invigorating air – this, despite the fact that, even in this warm climate, winter has this year been much less mild than usual. I felt there that I was quite alone, or at least not known to those people who passed by, but hardly had I got home when Michele, who had come up to see to the fire in my room, told me that a certain man, almost a beggar, who had turned up a short while earlier at that wretched inn, asked him if I was the young man who had once studied in Padua. He could not give my name, but he knew many facts about me and those times, and he did mention you by name. Michele went on to say, 'I was quite baffled. All the same, I told him he was correct. He was speaking Venetian, and

101

anyway it is a pleasant thing to find a compatriot in this solitude. But then he is so ragged! In short, I promised him – this may displease you, sir, but I felt so very sorry for him – I promised him he could see you. Indeed, he is outside now.' I told Michele to bring him in, and while I waited I felt myself overcome by a sudden sadness. The servant came back with a tall, emaciated man. He seemed young and handsome, but it was difficult to tell because his face was lined with grief. O my brother! There I was, wrapped in furs and sitting by the fire. My thick winter-cloak was lying idle on the chair nearby. The innkeeper was going to and fro getting my lunch ready, and that wretch was wearing only a linen jacket. And it made me cold just to look at him. I think the sadness of my welcome and his own miserable state may have disheartened him at first, but then, after I had spoken a few words, he realised that your Jacopo is not one to dishearten those who are unfortunate. He sat down with me to warm himself, and told me how he had spent this last unhappy year. He said, 'I was on familiar terms with a student who was with you night and day in Padua.' And he named you. 'It is a long time now since I had any news of him, but I hope that fate is not too harsh with him. I used to be a student then.' I shall not tell you, Lorenzo, who he is. Would it be right for me to sadden you with the misfortunes of someone whom you knew when he was happy, and whom you may still love? It is too much already that fate has condemned you to be constantly afflicted over me.

He continued, 'When I was coming today from Albenga, before I reached the village, I came across you by the seashore. You didn't notice how I kept turning round to look at you. I thought I recognised you, but since I knew you only by sight, and that was four years ago, I thought I might be mistaken. Your servant confirmed that I was right.'

I thanked him for coming to see me. I spoke to him about you, and I said he was all the more welcome to me because he mentioned Lorenzo's name. I shall not repeat to you his grievous account. He emigrated after the Peace of Campoformio, and enrolled as a lieutenant in the Cisalpine artillery. When he complained one day of the labours and vexations which he had to bear, a friend offered him a job. He left the militia. But neither the friend, nor the job, nor a home were to be found. He eked out a miserable existence through Italy, and embarked at Leghorn. But while he was speaking, I heard from the neighbouring room a baby crying and a low lament, and I noticed that he was pausing every so often to listen to it, and with some anxiety. And when the crying stopped, he went on. 'Perhaps,' I said to him, 'they are travellers who have just arrived.' 'No,' he replied, 'it is my little daughter of thirteen months who is weeping.'

He went on to tell me that while he was a lieutenant he married a girl in poor circumstances, and that the perpetual marches, which the young woman could not endure, and the poor wages had driven him to confide in the man who had betrayed him. From Leghorn he sailed to Marseille, trusting to luck, and he made his way right through Provence. And then through the Dauphiné, trying to teach Italian, without ever managing to find either work or bread. And now he was returning from Avignon to Milan. 'I look back,' he continued, 'at the time that is gone, and don't know how it can have passed like this for me. Without money, always followed by an exhausted wife with lacerated feet, her arms weary with the weight of an innocent creature always in need of nourishment from the drained breasts of her mother, and wringing the hearts of her wretched parents with her cries, while we cannot calm her down by explaining the reason for our misfortunes. How many burning days, how many freezing nights we have slept with the pack-animals in their sheds, or like the beasts in caves! Driven from town to town by every government, either because my poverty kept the magistrates' doors closed to me, or because no one took account of me. And those who knew me, either did not wish to know me, or turned their backs on me.' 'Yes, indeed,' I said, 'I know that in Milan and elsewhere many of our fellow-citizens who have emigrated are regarded as liberals.' 'Well then,' he went on, 'my misfortune has made them particularly cruel to me. Even the kindest people get tired of doing good: there are so many unfortunates! I don't know. But so-and-so, and so-and-so…' (The names of those men whom I found to be such hypocrites were, Lorenzo, so many knives thrust into my heart.) 'One made me wait at his door again and again to no purpose. One, after promising me so much, made me walk miles to his holiday home, and then spared me just a few coppers. The most humane threw me a crust of bread without bothering to see me. The most munificent made me, ragged as I was, pass through an assembly of friends and guests, and after reminding me of the decline of my family's prosperity, and of the need for diligence and probity, told me in a friendly way to return early the next morning. When I did return, I found three servants in the anteroom. One of them told me that his master was asleep, then he put two *scudi* and a shirt into my hands. Oh sir, I don't know if you are rich, but your appearance and your sighs tell me you are unlucky and pitiful. Believe me, I know by experience that money can make even a usurer seem beneficent, and that a great lord seldom deigns to invest his generosity in rags.'

I was silent. He rose and, as he took his leave, he went on to say, 'Books taught me that I should love mankind and virtue. But books, mankind, and virtue have all betrayed me. My head has learning, my heart is full of indignation, and my arms are incapable of any useful work. Could my father only hear, from the earth where he lies buried, with what heaviness of heart I blame him for not having made his five sons carpenters or tailors! Through his wretched vanity of wanting to preserve nobility without a fortune, he has, for all our sakes, squandered what little he possessed on the university and the *beau monde*. And what has become of us? I have never discovered what happened to my brothers. I have written often, but I have had no reply. They must be either wretched or unnatural. As for me, you see the fruit of my father's hopes and ambitions. How often have I been driven, either by nightfall or by hunger, to take shelter in an inn. But as I entered I did not know how I would pay the reckoning the next day. Without shoes, without clothes.' 'Oh, have some clothes,' I said, and I threw my winter-cloak on him. And Michele, who having come into the room to perform some task or other had paused nearby in order to listen, approached us wiping his eyes with the back of his hand, and adjusted the cloak upon his back. He did this with a certain respect, as though he was afraid of insulting the fallen estate of such a well-born person.

O Michele! I recall that you have had the possibility of living as a free man ever since the day your elder brother opened a shop and asked you to work with him, and yet you chose to remain with me, although that meant you were a servant. I am aware of the gracious respect with which you conceal my caprices, and do not insist you are right when I am angry and unjust. And I see how merrily you get along amidst all the irritations of my solitude, and I see how faithfully you bear all the troubles of my pilgrimage. Your jovial countenance often calms me down, but when I am silent whole days together, overcome by a black mood, you repress the joy that is in your heart, content not to make me even more aware of my state. And your kindness to that unfortunate person has sanctified my gratitude to you. You are the son of my wet-nurse, and you were brought up in my home. I shall never forsake you. But I love you all the more because I realise that your condition as a servant might have hardened your kind disposition if you had not been nurtured by my tender mother, by that lady who, with her delicacy of mind and her sweet ways, makes all who live with her courteous and loving.

When I was alone I gave Michele all I could spare, and he, while I dined, took it to that poor wretch. I left myself scarcely enough to get me to Nice, where I could exchange the bills which I had had forwarded from the bank at Genoa to Toulon and Marseille. This morning he came with his wife and child to thank me before he left, and I saw with what joy he kept repeating, 'Without you I would today have been looking for the first hospital.' I did not have the strength to reply to him, but my heart was saying, 'Now you have enough to live on for four months, six perhaps, and then? It is deceptive hope which is leading you by the hand, and the pleasant avenue which you are entering may take you onto a more disastrous path. You were looking for the nearest hospital, and you may not have been far from the shelter of the grave. But the little aid which I have afforded (my own fate does not allow me to help you further) will give you fresh vigour to bear once more and for a longer time those ills which have already almost consumed you and freed you for ever. Meanwhile, enjoy the present moment. But what hardships you must have endured when this state, which to many would be a troubled one, seems to you so joyful! Ah, if you were not a father and a husband, I should perhaps give you some advice!' And without saying a word I embraced him, and as they went away I looked after them and felt that my heart was breaking.

Last night as I was undressing I wondered, 'Why did that man ever leave his homeland? Why did he get married? Why did he give up secure employment?' And his whole history seemed to me like the story of a madman. And I tried to think what he could have done or not done to avoid being overcome by all those disasters. But since I have often heard such questions repeated fruitlessly, and have seen how good everyone is at coping with other people's problems, I fell asleep mumbling, 'O mortals who regard as imprudent all those who are not prosperous, put your hands on your hearts and then say truly whether you yourselves are wiser, or simply luckier?'

Now do you believe that everything he said was true? Do I? I believe that he was half-naked, and I was clothed. I saw an ailing wife. I heard a baby crying. Lorenzo, people go looking high and low for faults in the man who is poor, because their consciences tell them that Nature has given him a right to the goods of the rich. What? You say that most misfortunes are the consequence of vices, and in the man we are considering they may even be the result of a crime? Maybe… but so far as I am concerned, I do not know, and I do not enquire. As a judge, I would condemn all criminals, but as a man, oh, I think of the horror with which the first idea of the crime is born, of the hunger and the passions which lead to its consummation, of the endless agonies, of the remorse with which the man satisfies his hunger with the bloodstained fruit of his guilt, of the prisons which the offender sees always wide open and ready to bury him. And if he escapes justice, only to pay the price with dishonour and poverty, should I abandon him to desperation and fresh crimes? Is he the only guilty one? Calumny, betrayal of secrets, seduction, malignity, black ingratitude are more atrocious crimes, but are they ever threatened with punishment? And many a man by his crimes has won honours in the field! O legislators, O judges, punish! But go occasionally into the hovels of the populace, and into the suburbs of all our capital cities, and every day you will see a quarter of the population wake up on beds of straw, not knowing where they are to find the simple necessities of life. I do realise that society cannot be changed, and I do know that starvation, crimes, and punishments are essential for social order and universal prosperity. The belief is that the world cannot keep going without judges and scaffolds, and I believe it because everyone else believes it. But I myself will never be a judge. In this vast land where the human race is born, lives, dies, reproduces itself, busies itself, and then ends up dying without knowing how or why, I can only distinguish those who are lucky and those who are unlucky. And if I meet someone who is unfortunate, I have compassion for our common lot. And I pour as much oil into the man's wounds as I can. But I leave his merits and his faults to be weighed by God.

VENTIMIGLIA, 19TH AND 20TH FEBRUARY

You are desperately unhappy, and you live in the agony of death, without its tranquillity. Nevertheless, you should endure all this for the sake of others. That is what Philosophy says, demanding of men a heroism from which Nature shrinks. Can the man who hates his own life love so much what little benefit it may give to society, that he will offer up years of distress to this illusion? And how can he have hope for others who has no desires or hopes for himself? He who, having been forsaken by others, has forsaken himself?

You are not the only one who is unhappy. How true! But isn't this consolation rather an instance of the secret envy of others' prosperity which is latent in everyone? Others' misery does not diminish mine. Who is so generous as to saddle himself with my misfortunes? Who, even if he wished to, could? He might have greater courage to bear them. But what use is courage without strength? That man who is swept away by the irresistible current of a swollen river is not therefore base. He is base rather who has the strength to save himself and does not use it. And who is so wise that he can be judge of our hidden strength? Who can draw up rules concerning the effects of their passions on the various temperaments of men and the effects of the incalculable circumstances in which they find themselves, rules by which we could decide: this man is a coward because he succumbs, that man who manages to endure is a hero? Since our instinctive love of life is so powerful, the former might well have fought more fiercely to survive than the latter did to endure.

But the debts which you owe to society? What debts? Debts incurred when society dragged me from my freedom in the lap of Nature, when I had neither the reasoning power nor the will to agree to this, nor the strength to oppose it, and brought me up amongst its needs and prejudices? Forgive me, Lorenzo, if I keep going over this matter which is such a bone of contention between us. I have no wish to make you change your opinion, which is so different from mine. I wish rather to dispel my own doubts. You would be as convinced as I am, if you felt my sorrows. May heaven spare you them! Have I contracted these debts naturally? And, like a slave, I must pay with my life for these ills which society provides for me, simply because society calls them benefits? And even if they are benefits, I enjoy them and pay for them as long as I live. And if when I am dead I am no use to society, what benefits do I get from society in the tomb? O my friend, every individual is a born enemy of society, because society is of necessity hostile to individuals. Put the case that all mortals had something to gain by abandoning their lives, do you believe that they would go on living for my sake alone? And if I commit an action which is harmful to the majority, I am punished, while I shall never be able to take my revenge for their actions, even when they redound to my great harm. They may well claim that I am the child of a great family; but I, renouncing both the benefits and the duties of the community, can say, 'I am a world in myself, and I mean to cut myself free because I lack the happiness which you promised.' If by separating myself I do not find my share of liberty, if men have taken it from me because they are stronger, if they punish me because I ask for it back – then do I not free them from their lying promises and from my impotent demands if I seek refuge in the tomb? Ah, those philosophers who have preached the Gospel of human virtue, natural honesty, and reciprocal benevolence are unintentional apostles of people who are cunning. And they seduce those few frank and ardent souls who, loving mankind sincerely in their eagerness to be loved in return, will always be victims repenting too late of their loyal credulity.

And yet so many times all these reasonable arguments have found no way into my heart, because I continued to hope I might consecrate my torments to the happiness of others! But for God's sake listen to me and answer me! What purpose have I in living? What use am I to you, being a fugitive in these cavernous mountains? What honour do I bring to myself, to my homeland, to my dear ones? Do these solitudes differ in any way from the tomb? My death would be for me the natural end of my troubles, and for all of you the end of your anxieties on my account. Instead of continual sufferings I would give you one sole grief – a tremendous one, but the last, and you would be assured of my eternal peace. Sorrow cannot buy life back.

And every day I think of the expense to which for some months I have put my mother. I don't know how she manages to cope. If I returned home, I would see our house bare of all its splendour. It was beginning to lose it long before I left, because of the public and private extortions which never ceased to afflict us. Nevertheless, that kindly woman does not cease to care. I found more money from her in Milan. But this affectionate generosity will certainly diminish the comforts among which she was born. She was indeed unfortunate in her marriage! Her own wealth maintains my home which was going to ruin through my father's prodigality; and her old age makes these thoughts all the more bitter to me. If she but knew! All her efforts are in vain for her unfortunate son. And if she could see inside me, if she could see the shadows which consume my soul! I beg you not to speak of them to her, Lorenzo. But is this life? Oh yes, I am still living, and all that animates my days is a dull hope which continues to enliven them, and which nevertheless I try not to hear. I do not succeed – and if I try to disabuse myself of this hope, it turns into a hellish desperation.

Your oath, Teresa, will be at the same time a sentence on me. And yet, so long as you are free, and so long as our love remains at the mercy of circumstances, of the future which is uncertain, and of death, you will always be mine. I speak to you, I look at you, and I embrace you, and I believe that even at this distance you feel the pressure of my lips, and are aware of my tears. But when your father offers you as a sacrifice of reconciliation on the altar of God, when you have restored peace to your family by your tears, well then at that point I – no, not I but desperation alone and of itself – will destroy the man and his passions. And how could my love be extinguished, while I live? And how will its sweet allurements ever fail to entice you in the secret depths of your heart? But then they can hardly be holy and innocent any longer. I shall not love, when she is another's, the lady who was mine. I love Teresa immensely, but not the wife of Odoardo. Alas, even as I write you may be in his bed! Lorenzo! O Lorenzo, this is the demon who haunts me. He is at my heels, he bears down on me, he attacks me, and he blinds my intellect, and he even stops my heart beating, and he fills me with ferocity, and he would like to see the world finish with me. *You all weep.*[19] And why does he shove a dagger into my hands, and go in front of me, and look back to see if I am following him, and point out to me the spot where I must strike? Are you here as an agent of the vengeance of highest heaven? And so in my frenzy and superstition I throw myself down in the dust horribly beseeching a God whom I do not know, whom at other times I honestly adored, whom I have not offended, of whom I always doubt. And then I tremble, and adore him. Where can I look for help? Not in myself, and not in other men. I have stained the earth with blood, and the sun is black.

Here at last I am at peace! But what kind of peace? The tiredness, the torpor of the tomb. I have wandered over these mountains. There is not a tree, not a hut, not a blade of grass. It is all bare, with gnarled bushes, rough, grey boulders, and many crosses scattered about which mark the spots where travellers have been assassinated. Over there is the Roia, a torrent which when the ice melts rushes from the entrails of the Alps, and for a long stretch splits this immense mountain in two. Near the coast there is a bridge which reunites the track. I stopped on that bridge, and looked as far as my eyes could see. Scanning the two sides of very high rocks and cavernous ravines, one can just about glimpse, on the peaks of the Alps, other snowy Alps which blend into the sky, and everything is white and blurred. From these Alps which have been split open, the north wind sinks and strolls in, undulating, and through these jaws it invades the Mediterranean. Nature takes her seat here, solitary and threatening, and drives all living beings from this realm of hers.

These, O Italy, are your borders! But every day they are crossed at every point by the obstinate greed of other nations. Where are your children then? You lack nothing but the strength which comes from a common purpose. I would indeed give my unhappy life gloriously for you. But what can be done by my arm alone, and by my mere voice? Where is the ancient terror your glory inspired? Wretches! We go on every day recalling the liberty and glory of our forefathers, who the more they shine the more they reveal our abject slavery. While we invoke those magnificent shades, our enemies trample over their tombs. And the day may come when, having lost our wealth and intellects and voices, we become like the household slaves of the ancients, or are sold like the poor Negroes, and see our masters open up the tombs of those Great Men, and exhume their ashes and scatter them to the winds in order to destroy even their memory. Today our monuments are an occasion of pride, but not enough to shake us out of our ancient lethargy.

That is what I exclaim when I feel my breast swell with pride at the thought of being Italian, and fail to find a homeland as I look inside myself. But then I say, 'It seems as though men are the authors of their own misfortunes, but these misfortunes arise from the way the universe is ordered, and so the human race in its pride and blindness is the instrument of the fates. We reason from what has happened over a few centuries. But what are they in the immense tracts of Time? Like the seasons of our mortal life, they seem at times to be full of extraordinary events, which are, however, only the normal and necessary effects of the nature of things. There is a balancing out in the universe. Nations devour each other because no single one of them could go on existing without the bodies of another. When I gaze at Italy from where I stand on these Alps, I weep and tremble, and I call for vengeance on the invaders. But my voice is lost in that murmur which is all that now survives of so many dead nations. When the Romans were plundering the world, they looked over seas and deserts for fresh empires which they might devastate, they violated the gods of the vanquished, and they threw princes and free peoples into chains, until, finding nowhere else to bloody their blades, they turned them against themselves. Just so the Israelites slaughtered the peaceful inhabitants of Canaan, and the Babylonians forced into slavery the priests, the mothers, and the little children of the people of Juda. Just so Alexander overthrew the empire of Babylon and, having laid waste a large part of the earth, wept that he had no more worlds to conquer. Just so the Spartans devastated Messenia three times, and three times drove the Messenians out of Greece, even though they were Greeks, of the same religion as themselves, and descendants of the same ancestors. Just so the ancient

Italians tore each other to pieces, until they were swallowed up by the success of Rome. But in a few centuries the Queen of the World became prey to Caesars, Neros, Constantines, Vandals, and Popes. Oh how much smoke from human pyres covered the sky of America, and how much blood of innumerable peoples, who inspired the Europeans with neither fear nor envy, was borne across the ocean to taint our shores with infamy! But that blood will one day be avenged and will be poured down on the sons of the Europeans! All nations have their moment. Today they are tyrants, only to bring about their own servitude tomorrow. And those who were once basely paying tribute, will one day impose that tribute with sword and fire. The world is a forest full of wild beasts. Hunger, floods, and plagues are simply measures taken by Nature, like a field lying barren which is prepared for abundance in the coming year. And who knows? Perhaps even the misfortunes of this globe of ours are preparations for the prosperity of another globe?

Meanwhile in our pomposity we call virtue all those actions which lead to the security of him who commands and the fear of him who serves. Governments impose justice. But could they impose it, if they had not first violated it in order to reign? He who in his ambition has stolen whole provinces solemnly sends to the gallows him who in hunger steals bread. So when brute force has violated all other people's rights, in order to preserve them afterwards for itself, it deceives mortals with the appearance of justice, until it is itself destroyed by another force. That is the way the world goes – and men. Meanwhile, from time to time, some bolder mortals arise, at first derided as madmen, and often beheaded as criminals. If they happen to be favoured by fortune – which they think is in their power, but which is ultimately only the irresistible movement of events – well then, they are obeyed and feared, and deified after death. This is the race of heroes, of heads of parties, and of founders of nations who, in their own pride and because of the stupidity of the crowd, think they have risen so high by their own worth. And they are mere cogs in the machine. When the time is ripe for a revolution in the world, there must of necessity be men who started it, and whose skulls make a footstool at the throne of him who finishes it. And because the human race finds neither happiness nor justice on this earth, men create gods to protect the weak, and they look for future rewards to make up for their present distress. But in every century the gods clothe themselves in the conquerors' arms, and they oppress the peoples with the passions, the rages, and the cunning of those who want to rule.

Do you know, Lorenzo, where virtue still lives? In us few weak and unhappy ones – in us who, having experienced all the mistakes and felt all the woes of life, know how to sympathise with them and relieve them. Compassion, you are the only true virtue! All the others look for some advantage or gain.

But while I am looking down from a great height upon the follies and fated misfortunes of humanity, do I not feel all the passions and the weakness and the weeping, all those elements which go to make up a man? Do I not sigh every day for my homeland? And I say to myself as I weep, 'You have a mother and a friend. You love. A throng of unhappy people are waiting for you, people to whom you are dear, and who have hopes for you. Where do you flee? Even in foreign lands you will be followed by men's perfidy and by griefs and death. It is possible you will die here, and no one will have pity on you. And in your unhappy breast you still take pleasure in being pitied. Abandoned by all, do you not ask heaven for help? Heaven does not listen, and yet in your afflictions your heart turns involuntarily to heaven. So go and prostrate yourself, but prostrate yourself before the domestic altars.'

O Nature! Can it be that you have need of us wretches, and think of us as you do of these worms and insects which swarm and multiply without knowing why they live? But, since you have granted us this fatal instinct for life which prevents us mortals from falling beneath the burden of our infirmities and makes us unfailingly obey all your laws, why do you give us the even more fatal gift of reason? We are deeply aware of all our calamities, without being able to do anything about them.

So why am I fleeing? In what distant lands can I lose myself? Where will I ever find men who are different from men? Do I not indeed foresee the disasters, the weaknesses, and the poverty which await me beyond the borders of my homeland? No, I shall go back to you, sacred earth which heard my first cries, where so often I have rested my tired limbs, where in obscurity and peace I have found my few delights, where in grief I have confessed my distress. Since everything for me is clothed in

sadness, I may at least still hope that the everlasting sleep of death…
You alone, O my woods, will hear my last lament, and you alone with
your tranquil shade will cover my cold corpse. I shall be mourned by
those unhappy ones who are the companions of my misfortune, and if
the passions live beyond the tomb, my sorrowful spirit will be comforted
by the sighs of that heavenly maiden who I believed was born for me,
but whom the interests of men and my savage destiny snatched from my
breast.

ALESSANDRIA, 29TH FEBRUARY

From Nice, instead of going further into France, I have taken the route
for Monferrato. Tonight I shall sleep in Piacenza. On Thursday I shall
write from Rimini. I shall explain everything then. For now, farewell.

RIMINI, 5TH MARCH

Everything is melting away from me. I came here anxious to see the poet
Bertola once more. For a long time I had had no letter from him. He is
dead.

ELEVEN O'CLOCK IN THE EVENING

I know. Teresa is married. You stay silent, not wishing to inflict on me
the final wound, but the man who is ill groans while death is attacking
him, not when death has conquered him. It is better like this, because
now it is all decided. And now I too am peaceful, incredibly peaceful.
Farewell. Rome will always be in my heart.

*From the following fragment, which is dated the same evening, it appears
that on that day Jacopo decided to die. Several other fragments, gathered
like this one from his papers, seem to be the last thoughts which confirmed
him in his resolution, and so I shall intersperse them according to their
dates.*

I have the end in sight. For a long time my mind has been made up. I
know the means and the place, and the day is not far distant.

What is life for me? Time has devoured my moments of happiness. I
only know that I am alive when I feel grief. And now even that illusion

abandons me. I think of the past; I concentrate on the days which are to come. And I see nothing. These years of my youth, how slowly they have passed among fears, hopes, desires, deceptions, boredom! And if I look for the inheritance they have left me with, I find only the remembrance of a few pleasures which are no more, and an ocean of misfortunes which make me quail, because they make me fear that there is worse to come. If in life there is grief, in what may we hope? In nothingness. Or in another life completely different from this one. And so I have made my decision. I do not hate myself in my despair. I do not hate the living. For a long time I have been searching for peace, and reason always directs me to the tomb. How often, sunk in meditation on my misfortunes, have I begun to despair of myself! Then the idea of death dispelled my sadness, and I found myself smiling in the hope of living no longer.

I am tranquil, tranquil to the point of imperturbability. My illusions have vanished. My desires are dead. My intellect has been freed from hopes and fears. No longer do a thousand phantasms, sometimes joyful, sometimes sad, confuse and mislead my imagination. No longer do empty arguments flatter my reason. I am completely calm. Repentance of the past, boredom in the present, and fear of the future. Such is human life. Only death, to which is committed the sacred transformation of everything, promises peace.

He did not write to me from Ravenna, but from this other passage it can be seen that he went there that week.

Not in a foolhardy way, but with a mind that is assured and well-advised. How many tempests before Death could speak so calmly with me – and I so calmly with him!

On your funeral urn, Father Dante![20] As I embraced it I became all the more determined. Did you see me? Father, did you not inspire me with such strength of mind and heart while I genuflected, with my forehead pressed against the marble of your tomb, and meditated on your high-mindedness, and your love, and your ungrateful native city, and your exile, and your poverty, and your divine intellect? I parted from your shade more resolved and more joyful.

At dawn on 13th March he went to the Euganean Hills, sent Michele to Venice, and all at once, booted as he was, threw himself down to sleep. I was with Jacopo's mother that very moment when she, seeing the servant before I did, asked in her fear, 'And what of my son?' The letter from Alessandria had not yet arrived, and Jacopo had anticipated even that from Rimini. We had been thinking that he was already in France. Therefore the unexpected return of his servant gave us a foreboding of grim news. He told us, 'The master is in the country. He cannot write, because we have been travelling all night. He was sleeping when I got on my horse. I have come to tell you that we are to set off again. I think, from what I have heard him say, that it will be for Rome. For Rome, if I remember correctly, and then for Ancona where we shall take ship. In addition I can tell you that the master is well. He has been cheerful for almost a week now. He told me that before he left he would come to say hello to you, signora, and so he has sent me to inform you. In fact, he will be here the day after tomorrow, perhaps even tomorrow.' The servant seemed to be happy, but his confused account increased our anxiety. And this anxiety was not relieved until the next day, when Jacopo wrote to say that he was about to leave for the once Venetian islands,[21] *and that, fearing he might never return, he would come to see us again and receive his mother's blessing. This note has been lost.*

Meanwhile, on the day of his arrival in the Euganean Hills, he awoke four hours before sunset, went for a walk as far as the church, returned, changed his clothes, and set out for the T*** home. He learned from a servant that they had all come from Padua six days before, and that at any moment they would return from their walk. It was almost evening, and he started to return home. He had only taken a few paces when he became aware that Teresa was coming along holding Isabella by the hand, and behind his daughters came Signor T*** with Odoardo. Jacopo was seized by a trembling, and approached them in an embarrassed way. As soon as she recognised him Teresa cried out, 'God in heaven!' She fell back, almost fainting, and caught hold of her father's arm for support. When Jacopo was near, and they all recognised him, she did not say a word. Signor T*** scarcely held out his hand, and Odoardo greeted him curtly. Only Isabella ran to him, and as he took her in his arms she kissed him, and called him her Jacopo, and turned round to point him out to Teresa. As he accompanied them he talked sotto voce with the little girl. No one opened his mouth, except Odoardo who asked him if he was going to Venice. 'In a few days,' he replied. When they reached the door he took his leave.

Michele, who would on no account rest in Venice and leave his master alone, returned to the hills about one hour after midnight, and found him seated at his writing-desk looking over his papers. Many of them he burned, and some of less importance he tore up and dropped under his desk. The servant went to bed, leaving the gardener to take care of things. Jacopo had not eaten the whole day. Soon afterwards part of his dinner was brought to him, and he actually ate some of it, although his attention was still with his papers. He did not examine them all, but he walked up and down his room, and then started to read. The gardener, who saw all this, told me that towards the end of the night he opened the windows, and paused by them for a while. It seems as if immediately afterwards he wrote these two fragments. They are on different sides of the same sheet.

Come on, be constant. There is a brazier before you, glittering with blazing coals. Stick your hand in it. Burn your living flesh, and take care that you do not disgrace yourself by groaning. But what is the point? What is the point of affecting a heroism which does me no good?

It is night, deep dark night. Why do I stay awake motionless over this book? I have learnt nothing but the ability to display wisdom while the passions are not tyrannising my soul. Precepts are like medicines – useless when the sickness overcomes all Nature's resistance.

Some sages boast of having conquered passions which they have never had to fight against. This is what lies behind their self-confidence. Beloved star of the dawn! You are blazing in the east, and sending to my eyes your rays – for the last time! Who would have said that six months ago, when you appeared before the other planets to gladden the night and receive our greetings?

If only dawn were breaking! Perhaps Teresa is remembering me at this moment – a consoling thought! Oh, how the blessedness of being loved can sweeten any grief whatsoever!

A mere delirium of the night! Away – you are starting to beguile me once again. Your time has gone. I am disabused of the illusion. Only one course remains to me.

In the morning he sent to Odoardo for a Bible. Odoardo did not have one. He sent to the parish priest, and when one was brought to him, he shut himself up with it. When midday was striking he went out to dispatch the following letter, and then went and shut himself up once more.

14TH MARCH

Lorenzo, I have for some months been guarding a secret in my heart; but the hour for departure is about to strike, and it is time for me to open my heart to you.

Your friend cannot stop thinking of a corpse! I have done my duty. The family has from that day not been so poor. But will that bring back their father?

One day – at the time when I was crazy with grief, ten months ago now – I went for a ride which took me many miles away. It was evening. I saw that bad weather was on its way, and I hurried as I returned. My horse ate up the miles, and still I bloodied his sides with my spurs. I let the reins rest loose upon his neck, almost as though I were inviting him to fall and kill us both. As we entered a very long, narrow, tree-lined avenue I saw someone. I caught hold of the reins again, but the horse became more furious and threw himself forward with greater impetuosity. 'Keep to the left,' I shouted, 'to the left!' The unfortunate man understood me. He ran to the left, but hearing the trampling come nearer, and thinking that the horse was already upon him in that narrow way, in his dismay he turned to the right, and was run down and knocked over, and the hooves shattered his skull. Such was the violence of the collision that the horse fell heavily, hurling me out of the saddle several yards away. Why was I still alive and unharmed? I ran to where I heard the wail of a dying man. He was breathing his last, face downward in a pool of blood. I shook him. He had no voice or feeling. In a few minutes he died.

I returned home. That night was indeed a stormy one. Hail laid the fields waste. Many trees were struck by lightning, and the wind smashed a wayside shrine with its crucifix. I was out all that night, my clothes and my soul covered with blood, trying to lose myself in the mountains, hoping to find in that destruction some punishment for my fault. What a night! Can you think that that terrible ghost has ever pardoned me? The following morning, it was much talked about. The dead man was found in that avenue, half a mile away, under a heap of stones between two broken chestnut trees which had fallen across the way; the rain, which had been coming down from the heights in torrents until dawn, had dragged him there together with those stones. His limbs and face were in shreds. His discovery was announced by the cries of his wife who was looking for him. No one was accused of the death. But in my heart I felt accused when I heard that widow blessing me because I had straightaway placed her daughter with the nephew of my steward, and given an allowance to her little son who wanted to become a priest. And yesterday evening they came again to thank me, saying that I had freed them from the poverty in which the family of that poor workman had languished for so many years. Ah, there are so many other wretches besides you, but they have a husband and father to comfort them with his love, and whom they would not exchange for all the riches of the earth. And you?

So men are born to be destroyed by each other!

All the peasants keep away from that avenue, and when they are coming back from their work, they go through the meadows to avoid it. They say that at night spirits are seen there, that the bird of ill omen perches in those trees and after midnight hoots three times, that some evenings a dead man has been seen walking there. And I dare not disabuse them. Nor dare I laugh at such absurdities. But after my death all shall be revealed. The journey is risky, and my health is uncertain. I cannot go away with this remorse buried within me. May those two small children, in all their misfortune, and that widow be always respected in my house. Farewell.

Many days later in the Bible were found, full of deletions and almost illegible, translations of some verses of the book of Job, of the second chapter of Ecclesiastes, and of the whole of the book of Ezekiel.

At four in the afternoon he found himself at the T*** home. Teresa *had gone quite alone into the garden. Her father received him affably. Nearby on a balcony Odoardo pretended to read. After a short while he put the book down. He opened another and made his way to his rooms reading it. Then Jacopo took up the first book just as it had been left open by Odoardo. It was volume IV of the tragedies of Alfieri. He glanced at one or two pages, then read in a loud voice:*

Who are you?… Who has spoken of the pure
And open air?… Like this? This is thick fog.
Shadows are here, and shades of death… Oh, look,
Come nearer. Do you see? The sun has round
Itself a garland of disastrous blood…
D'you hear the song sung by ill-omened birds?
A dismal sound of mourning fills the air
And strikes my ears, compelling me to weep…
But what is this? You too, are you too weeping?…[22]

Teresa's father looked at him and said, 'O my son!' Jacopo went on reading quietly. He opened the same volume at random, and putting it down quickly, he exclaimed:

I have not given you
Proof of my courage yet. But it will be
Great as my grief.[23]

At these verses Odoardo returned, and hearing them pronounced so effectively, paused at the door in thought. Signor T*** told me that he felt, in that moment, that he could read death on our unhappy friend's face, and that in those days all his words inspired reverence and pity. They then spoke of his journey, and when Odoardo asked him if it would be long before he returned, 'Yes,' he replied, 'I could almost swear that we shall not see each other again.' 'Not see each other again?' asked Signor T*** in a voice full of torment. Then Jacopo, as if to reassure him, looked him in the face with an expression that was both joyful and tranquil. And after a short silence, he smiled and recited that passage of Petrarch:

I do not know, perhaps
you will live very long on earth without me.[24]

Returning home at dusk, he shut himself away, and did not reappear outside his room until very late the following day. I include here some fragments which I believe he wrote that night, although I cannot say for certain exactly at what time they were written.

Cowardice? You who cry cowardice, are you not one of those innumerable mortals who look lazily at their chains, not daring to weep, and kiss the hand that scourges them? What is man after all? Courage has always dominated the universe because weakness and fear are everywhere.

You impute cowardice to me, and yet you sell your soul and your honour.

Come, look at me on the point of death, as I gasp in my own blood. Do you not tremble? Who is the coward now? But draw this knife from my breast, grasp it, and ask yourself, *'Must I live for ever?'* A very great pain, but short and magnificent. Who knows? Fortune has a more grievous and infamous death waiting for you. Confess. Now that you are deliberately holding that sharp weapon over your heart, do you not feel you are capable of any great enterprise, and do you not feel yourself to be free and the master of your tyrants?

MIDNIGHT

I look at the countryside. What a clear and peaceful night! There is the moon rising behind the mountain. O moon, friendly moon! Are you at this moment shining on Teresa's face with your rays full of pathos, like those rays which you radiate throughout my soul? I have always greeted you as you rose to comfort the silent solitude of the earth. Often as I came from Teresa's house I have spoken with you, and you were a witness to my fits of delirium. These tear-stained eyes have often accompanied you in the lap of the clouds that hid you. They have searched for you in the nights which were blind without your rays. You will rise again, you will rise again always more beautiful. But your friend will fall a disfigured corpse, never to rise again. I pray now for one last blessing from you. When Teresa goes looking for me among the cypresses and pines on the hill, may your rays illuminate my tomb.

What a lovely dawn! It is indeed a long time since I rose from such a restful sleep, and since I saw you, O morning, shining so brightly! But my eyes have always been full of weeping, and all my thoughts in darkness, and my soul was plunged in grief.

Shine out, shine out, O Nature, and cheer mortals up despite their anxieties. You will shine no more for me. I have already experienced all your beauty, and adored you, and I have been nourished by your joy. And so long as I saw you beautiful and beneficent you said to me in your divine voice: 'Live!' But in my desperation I saw you with hands dripping with blood. The fragrance of your flowers was for me impregnated with poison, your fruits were bitter, and you seemed to me to be the devourer of your children, luring them with your beauty and your blessings to grief.

Will I therefore be ungrateful to you? Will I protract my life in order to see you so terrible, and curse you? No, no. Transforming yourself, and blinding me with your light, are not you yourself abandoning me, and commanding me at the same time to abandon you? Ah, now I look at you and sigh, but I dream of you still because I remember past pleasures, and because I am certain I shall no more have to fear you, and because I am about to lose you. And yet I do not think I am rebelling against you when I flee from my life. Life and death are equally your laws. Indeed you allow us only one way to be born, but a thousand ways to die. If you do not blame us for the infirmity which kills us, would you blame us for the passions which have the same effect, and the same source since they both derive from you, and which could not oppress us if they had not received from you the strength to do it? Nor have you appointed a definite age for everyone to live. Men must be born, live, and die. Those are your laws. What do the time and the manner matter?

I am taking away nothing from what you have given me. My body, this infinitesimal part, will always be joined with you under other forms. My spirit, if it dies with me, it will be altered with me in the enormous scheme of things; and if it is immortal, its essence will remain unharmed!

Oh, what is the point of trying to deceive my reason any longer? Do I not hear the solemn voice of Nature? *I caused you to be born so that you would, in longing for your own felicity, conspire to bring about universal felicity, and therefore I gave you an instinctive love of life and an instinctive horror of death. But if the fullness of grief overcomes instinct, what else can you do but run and take the ways which I make smooth for you, the ways by which you may flee from your misfortunes? What gratitude do you owe to me, if the life which I gave you as a blessing has been changed for you into suffering?*

What arrogance! To believe that I am necessary! My years are, in the unlimited space of time, but an imperceptible instant. Think of rivers of blood which bear upon their reeking waves fresh heaps of the slain. And these millions of men are sacrificed for a few thousand yards of land, and for half a century of renown over which two conquerors fight with the lives of their peoples. And am I afraid of sacrificing to myself those few sad days which may well be snatched from me by the persecution of men, or polluted by faults?

I searched religiously for any traces I could find of my friend in his last hours, and just as religiously I am writing of what I have been able to find. However, I am telling you, dear reader, only what I saw or what was told to me by one who saw it. For all my efforts, I do not know what he did on 16th, 17th, and 18th March. He was many times at the T*** home, but he never stopped there. He went out every day almost before dawn, and he retired very late. He ate without saying a word, and Michele assures me that his nights were very peaceful.

The letter which follows does not have a date, but it was written on the nineteenth.

Am I imagining things, or is Teresa avoiding me? She is avoiding me! They all are. And Odoardo is always at her side. I should like to see her just once, and believe me I would have gone away already – and you keep on hurrying me more and more – if I had been able to bathe her hand in tears just once. There is a great silence throughout that family! As I climb the stairs I am afraid of meeting Odoardo. When he speaks to me, he never mentions Teresa. And also he is hardly polite! Always, as he did just now in fact, he asks me when and how I shall be leaving. I drew back from him quickly, because it really seemed to me that he was sneering, and I fled away trembling.

That terrible truth which I once discovered with horror returns to terrify me, although I have since become used to meditating on it resignedly: *We are all enemies.* If you could follow the train of thought of anyone who appears before you, you would see that he is waving a sword about to keep everyone away from his goods, and to seize other people's. Lorenzo, I am starting to vacillate once more. But I must get ready – and leave them in peace.

P.S. Coming back to that decrepit lady whom I believe I once mentioned to you – the sad creature is still alive! Alone, and abandoned, for whole days often, by all those who are tired of helping her, she is still alive. But for many months all her senses have been caught up in the horror and struggle of death.

Two fragments follow which may have been written that night, and they seem to be the last.

Let us tear the mask off that spectre which is trying to frighten us. I have seen children shudder and hide away from the distorted faces of their nurses. O Death! I look at you and I question you. It is not things themselves but their appearances which trouble us. Innumerable men who do not dare invoke you, nevertheless face you undaunted! Also you are a necessary part of Nature. By now you hold no more terror for me. To me you are like a sleep in the evening, rest after labour. Look at the spurs of that bare rock which cheat the valleys below them of the sun's fecund rays. To what purpose do I linger? If to cooperate for the sake of others' happiness, all I do is trouble them. If to bear that portion of calamity which is assigned to every man, I have already in twenty-four years emptied the cup which would have sufficed for a long life. And hope? What does that amount to? Have I such knowledge of the future as to entrust myself to it? Oh, it is just this fatal ignorance which flatters our passions, and nourishes human unhappiness.

Time flies, and with time I have lost in grief that element in my life which two months previously gave me an illusion of consolation. This inveterate wound has by now become part of my being. I feel it in my heart, in my brain, throughout the whole of myself. It drips blood, and it sighs as though it were freshly opened. This is enough, Teresa, enough. Do you not see in me a sick man dragging his feet to the tomb in desperation and torment, who cannot by a single blow forestall the agony of his inevitable destiny?

I test the point of this dagger. I clutch this dagger, and smile. Here, right in this throbbing heart – and it will all be finished. But this steel is always in front of me! Who, who dares to love you, Teresa? And who dared to carry you off? Flee from me then. Do not come near me, Odoardo! Oh! I am always rubbing my hands to wash away the spots of his blood. I sniff my hands as if they reeked of crime. And yet here they are, quite clean and ready to snatch me in an instant out of the danger of living one day more – one single day, one moment! Wretch, I would still have lived too long!

20TH MARCH, IN THE EVENING

I was being strong, but this was the final blow which almost destroyed my steadfastness! However, what is decreed is decreed. But you, my God, who see deeply into things, you see that this is a sacrifice of more than blood.

She was, Lorenzo, with her little sister, and it looked as if she was trying to avoid me. But then she sat down, and Isabella, full of distress, came and sat on her knee. 'Teresa,' I said to her, coming near and taking her hand. She looked at me, and that child, throwing her arm round Teresa's neck and looking up at her, said to her in an undertone, 'Jacopo does not love me any more.' And I heard her. 'I do not love you?' And bending down and embracing her, 'I love you,' I said to her, 'I love you dearly, but you will not see me again.' O my brother, Teresa looked at me in terror, clutching Isabella but keeping her eyes fixed upon me. 'You will leave us,' she said, 'and this little girl will be the companion of my days, and a comfort in my sufferings. I shall always speak to her of her friend – of my friend. And I shall teach her to weep and bless you.' At these final words it seemed to me that some hope was restored to her soul, and the tears rained from her eyes, and I write to you with hands still warm from that weeping. 'Farewell,' she added, 'farewell, but not for ever.' 'What are you saying? Not for ever?' 'Look, I am keeping my promise to you.' And she drew her portrait from her bosom. 'I am keeping my promise to you. Farewell. Go, go away, and take with you a keepsake of this unhappy woman. It is bathed in my tears and my mother's tears.' And with her own hands she hung it round my neck and hid it in my bosom. I stretched out my arms, and clutched her to my heart, and her sighs gave comfort to my burning lips, and my mouth was already… But the pallor of death was on her face, and while she pushed me away, I touched her hand and felt it cold and trembling, and with a weak and choking voice she said to me, 'Have pity! Farewell.' And she threw herself on the sofa, tightly clutching Isabella who was weeping with us. Her father came in, and our wretched state must surely have embittered his remorse.

He returned that evening so upset that Michele was afraid of something terrible happening. He resumed his examination of his papers, and he had many of them burned without reading them. Before the Revolution he had written a commentary on the Venetian Government in a style that was antiquated and authoritative, with an epigraph from Lucan: Jusque datum sceleri.[25] *One evening the year before he had read to Teresa the story of Lauretta, and Teresa said to me then that those rambling thoughts, which he sent to me with his letter of 29th April, were not the beginning of the story. Instead, they had been extracted from that little book he had completed, in which he described in detail what had happened to Lauretta, in a less passionate style. He did not spare either these or any other of his writings. He used to read very few books, think a great deal, flee suddenly from the seething tumult of the world into solitude, and then write out of the need to relieve his feelings. But all I have left is his Plutarch crammed with notes, with various sheets inserted containing discourses, and one very long discourse on the death of Nicias, and a Tacitus, with many extracts – including the whole second book of the Annals, and a large part of the second book of the Histories – translated by him with great care, and patiently recopied in the margins in very tiny letters. The fragments included above I picked out from torn sheets which he had thrown under his table as though they were of no account, and to which I have assigned the probable dates. But the following passage – whether the ideas in it are his or someone else's I do not know, but the style is all his – was written at the end of* The Thoughts of Marcus Aurelius, *under the date 3rd March 1794, and then I found it recopied at the end of his Tacitus under the date 1st January 1797. And near to this was the date 20th March 1799, five days before he died. Here is the passage:*

I do not know why I came into the world, or how, or what the world is, or what I am myself. And if I rush to investigate it I come back confused and in an ignorance which is more and more alarming. I do not know what my body is, my senses, my soul. And this very part of me which determines what I write, and which meditates on everything and on itself, can never be known. It is in vain that I try to measure in my mind these immense spaces of the universe which surround me. I find myself as it were attached to a small corner of an incomprehensible space, without knowing why I am situated here rather than elsewhere, or why this brief time of my existence is assigned to this moment in eternity rather than to one of all those which preceded it or which will follow. Everywhere I look I see nothing but infinity absorbing me like an atom.

On the night of 20th March, when he had gone over his papers again, he called the gardener and Michele to clear them all out of his way. Then he sent them to bed. It seems that he stayed awake all night, because it was then that he wrote the preceding letter, and around dawn the next day he went to wake the servant up, and told him to find a messenger for Venice. Then he stretched out fully dressed on the bed. But it was only for a short time, for a peasant told me he had met him at eight o'clock that morning on the Arquà road. Before midday he had gone back to his apartments. Michele came in to say that the messenger was there ready, and he found Jacopo sitting quite still, as though buried in very sad thoughts. He rose, went near to the window, and standing up he composed the following letter, in writing that was almost illegible:

I shall come in any case – if I could write to her – and I wished to write. Even if I wrote to her, I would not have the heart to come – you will tell her that I shall come, that she will see her son… nothing else – nothing else. Do not cause her any more suffering. I should have much to suggest to you about the way you ought to behave with her and comfort her in the future, but my lips are dry; I am choking. Such bitterness, such tightening of the chest – could I only breathe! There is a lump in my throat, and a hand is pressing on me and squeezing my heart. But, Lorenzo, what more can I say to you? I am a man. Oh my God, my God, just for today grant me the relief of tears.

He sealed the letter and handed it over without addressing it. He looked up at the sky for a long time. Then he sat down, and folding his arms on his desk, he laid his head down on them. His servant asked him again and again if he wanted anything else. Without turning round, he shook his head in denial. That day he began the following letter for Teresa.

WEDNESDAY, FIVE O'CLOCK

Resign yourself to heaven's decrees, and you will find some happiness in domestic peace, and in your harmony with that husband whom fate has destined for you. You have a father who is warm-hearted and unhappy. You should reunite him with your mother, who in her solitude and grief must be calling out to you alone. Your life depends on your good name. I alone, I alone in dying shall find peace, and I shall leave your home in peace. But you poor unhappy girl!

For many days now I have started to write to you without being able to continue! O God in heaven, I see that you do not forsake me in my last hour. This constancy is the greatest of your gifts to us. I shall die when I have received my mother's blessing and the last embrace of my friend. Your father will have your letters in his possession, and you will give him mine also. They will bear witness to the sanctity of our love. No, my dear young friend, you are not the cause of my death. All my desperate passions, the misfortunes of those people most necessary to my life, human crimes, the certainty of my perpetual slavery and of the perpetual infamy of my betrayed homeland – all had been decided a long time ago. And you, angelic as you are, could only mitigate my destiny, but never placate it! In you alone I saw the remedy for all my ills, and I dared to delude myself. And since you were irresistibly compelled to love me, my heart believed you were all mine. You have loved me, and you still love me – and now that I am losing you I call upon death to help me. Beg your father not to forget me, not so that he should be afflicted, but rather to soften your grief with his pity, and to make him remember he has another daughter.

But you, true friend to this unfortunate man, will never find it in your heart to forget me. Reread continually these last words of mine which I can vouch are written in my heart's blood. My memory may preserve you from the disasters which come with vice. Your beauty, your youth, the greatness of your fortune will all be incitements for others, for you, to stain that innocence to which you have sacrificed your first dear passion, and which has always been your one comfort in your sufferings. All that is flattering in the world will conspire to ruin you, to take away your self-respect, and to confound you with that horde of so many other women who, having renounced all shame, traffic in love and friendship, and display as trophies the victims of their perfidy. But this is not for you, my Teresa. Your virtue shines out from your heavenly face, and I have respected it. And you know that I have loved you and adored you as a sacred thing.

This divine image of my friend! Her last precious gift! As I look at it, it gives me new strength, and tells me all the story of our love. You were drawing this portrait the first day that I saw you. One by one all those days pass in front of me. They were the most troubled and the dearest days of my life. And you consecrated this portrait, fastening it to my breast bathed in your tears. And so, attached to my breast, it will accompany me to the tomb. You recall, Teresa, the tears with which I received it? Oh, I begin to shed them again, and they comfort my sad soul. If any life remains after my last sigh, it will be saved for you alone, and my love will live with me for ever. Meanwhile, hear one single, final, most sacred exhortation. I implore you by our unhappy love, by the tears which we have shed, by the respect which you feel for your parents, for whom you are a willing sacrificial victim – do not leave my poor mother unconsoled. She may well come to lament for me with you in this solitude, looking for some shelter from the storms of life. You alone are worthy to pity her and comfort her. Who is left, if you forsake her? In her anguish, in all her misfortunes, in the infirmity of her old age remember always that she is my mother.

At midnight he left the Euganean Hills by post-horse. Arriving at the sea at eight o'clock in the morning, he took a gondola to Venice and his home. When I arrived there, I found him asleep on a sofa, and sleeping peacefully. When he awakened he asked me to dispatch some matters of business for him, and to settle a debt of his at a certain bookseller's. He said to me, 'I can only stay here for today.'

Although it was almost two years since I had seen him, his face did not seem to me to have changed as much as I had expected. But then I noticed that he was walking slowly as though he had to drag himself along. His voice, which had once been quick and masculine, issued with difficulty and from deep within his breast. Nevertheless, he did his best to hold some conversation, and in replying to his mother who was questioning him about his journey, he frequently smiled a sad smile which was all his own. But he had an air of caution which was not like him. When I told him that some of his friends were coming that day to say hello to him, he answered that he did not wish to see a living soul ever again. In fact he himself went down to the door to instruct the servants to say that he would not receive any visitors. And when he came back he said to me, 'I've often thought that I shouldn't cause either you or my mother so much distress, but I still had an obligation and a need to see you again, and – believe me – it is a hard test of my courage.'

Some hours before evening he got up as if to leave, but his heart would not suffer him to say so. His mother drew near to him and, as he rose from his chair and went towards her with his arms wide open, she said with a resigned expression on her face, 'You are resolved then, my dear child?'

'Yes, yes,' he replied, embracing her and keeping his tears back with difficulty.

'Who knows if I shall see you again? I am old and weary now.'

'We may see each other again. My dear mother, take comfort, for we shall see each other again – never to part. But now – Lorenzo can bear witness to it.'

In her fear she turned to me, and I said to her, 'It is only too true.' And I told her how the persecution was becoming more intense because of the impending war. And that I was in danger too, mainly because of those letters of ours which had been intercepted (and these suspicions were not unwarranted, because a few months later I was obliged to forsake my homeland). And then she cried out, 'Go on living, my son, even if you are far away from me. Since your father's death I have not had one hour of well-being. I hoped that you would be a comfort to me in my old age, but the Lord's will be done! Go on living! I choose to be without you and weep, rather than see you imprisoned, or dead.' Her words were drowned in sobs.

Jacopo squeezed her hand, and looked at her as though he wanted to entrust a secret to her, but he quickly pulled himself together, and asked her for her blessing.

And she raised her hands: 'I bless you. I bless you, and may it please God Almighty to bless you too.'

By the stairs they embraced. That unhappy woman rested her head on her son's breast.

They went downstairs, and I with them. His mother, when she came to the door of the house and saw the open air, raised her eyes and held them fixed on the heavens for two or three minutes, and she seemed to be praying silently with all the fervour of her soul, and that act seemed to restore her former resignation. Without shedding further tears, she blessed her son again in a firm voice, and he kissed her hand again, and kissed her face.

I was weeping. After he had embraced me, he promised to write to me, and started to walk away, saying, 'When you are with my mother you will hold our friendship in pious memory.' Turning once more to his mother, he looked at her for a while without saying anything, and then he left. When he reached the end of the street he turned, waved his hand to us, and gazed at us sadly, as if he wanted to indicate that that was his final glance.

His poor mother stayed by the door, as if hoping that he would come back to her. But tearing her eyes away from the spot where he had disappeared from sight, she leant on my arm and said to me as we went back up, 'Dear Lorenzo, my heart tells me that we shall not see him ever again.'

An old priest who was on terms of familiarity with the Ortis family, and who had been Jacopo's Greek teacher, arrived that evening and told us how Jacopo had gone to the church where Lauretta was buried. Finding it closed, he desired the bell-ringer to open it at all costs, and he tipped a local lad to go and seek out the sacristan who had the keys. He sat waiting on a stone in the graveyard. Then he got up and leant his head against the door of the church. It was almost evening. When he became aware that there were people in the graveyard he waited no longer and went away. The old priest had got to know of all this from the bell-ringer. I learned some days later that towards nightfall Jacopo had gone to visit Lauretta's mother. 'He was very sad,' she told me. 'He did not speak at all of my poor daughter, and I didn't mention her, not wanting to wound him further. As he was going down the stairs he asked me to go when I could and comfort his mother.'

Meanwhile his mother that evening had a terrifying presentiment. Last autumn I was in the Euganean Hills and I read in the house of Signor T*** part of a letter in which Jacopo returned in thought to his paternal solitude. And then Teresa had depicted in chiaroscuro the view of Five Springs Lake, showing her friend on the slope of a little hill, stretched out on the grass and contemplating the setting of the sun. She asked her father for a line of verse as an inscription, and he suggested to her that line of Dante: 'He looks for freedom, such a precious thing.'[26]

Then she sent the little picture as a present to Jacopo's mother, begging her never to tell him where it came from. Indeed, he had never got to know. But that day when he was in Venice he noticed the picture hanging up, and saw who had drawn it. He did not say anything about it, but when he was quite alone in the room, he removed the glass, and below the line: 'He looks for freedom, such a precious thing, he wrote the one which follows it: 'As they know who give up their lives for it.'

And between the glass and the groove in the frame he found a long braid of hair which Teresa, some days before her marriage and without anyone knowing, had cut off and concealed in the frame in such a way that it could not be seen. When Jacopo saw that braid he put a lock of his own hair with it, and knotted the two together with the black ribbon he carried attached to his watch, and he put the picture back in its place. Some hours later his mother saw the line which he had added. She noticed *also the braid and the lock of hair and the black knot, which out of carelessness or haste he had not managed to hide completely. The following day she told me of it, and I saw how this event had shaken the courage with which she had previously borne her son's departure.*

So to soothe her I decided to go with him to Ancona, and I promised to write to her every day. He meanwhile returned to Padua, and stopped off at the home of Professor C***, where he slept for the rest of the night. When he was leaving in the morning the Professor showed him letters for some gentlemen, former pupils of his, who were from the once Venetian islands. Jacopo neither accepted the letters nor refused them. He returned on foot to the Euganean Hills, and began writing once more.

FRIDAY, ONE O'CLOCK

And you, Lorenzo, my loyal and one and only friend, forgive me. I do not need to commend my mother to you. I know well that she will have in you another son. But, O my mother, you will no longer have the son on whose breast you hoped to lay your white head. Nor will you be able to warm these dying lips with your kisses! And perhaps you will follow me! I have faltered, Lorenzo. Is this then her recompense after twenty-four years of hopes and care? So be it! God, who has ordained everything, will not forsake her. Nor will you! Ah, so long as my only desire was for a faithful friend, I lived happily. May heaven reward you! But you did not expect that I would reward you with tears. Alas, one way or another I shall repay you with tears. But do not utter over my ashes the cruel blasphemy: *He who wishes to die loves no one.* What didn't I take upon myself? What didn't I do? What did I not say to God? Woefully, all my life is in my passions. And if I could not destroy them with myself, what anguish, what agonies, what dangers, what fury, what lamentable blindness, what crimes would they not drag me into by force? One day, Lorenzo, before I had decided to die, I was genuflecting and imploring heaven to pity me, and my tears were flowing – and at that moment my tears suddenly dried up, and my heart grew fierce, and you would have thought that heaven itself had sent a delirium to attack me. And I stood up, and I wrote to that unhappy girl that I was going away to wait for her in another world, and that she should not delay to come to me. And I taught her how and when and the exact hour. But then it was not compassion, or shame, or remorse, or God himself, but rather the thought that she was no longer the virgin of two months ago, and that she was a woman polluted by the embrace of another, which made me repent of such an atrocious design. You can see how my life would be to all of you more grievous than my death, and even perhaps abominable to you all. If, on the other hand, I separate myself from Teresa for ever, while I am still worthy of her, her heart, still worthy of me, will certainly keep the memory of me, and although she is another's servant she will at least be able to hope – perhaps an utterly vain hope – that one day her soul will be free to unite for ever with mine. But farewell. Please give all these papers to her father. Gather my books together and preserve them in memory of your Jacopo. Take Michele in. I leave him my watch, what little furniture I have, and the cash which you will find in the small drawer of my writing-desk. Make sure you are alone when you open it. There is a letter in it for Teresa, which I beg you to give to her yourself. Farewell, farewell.

He continued the letter to Teresa.

I turn once more to you, my Teresa. If while I lived you were at fault in listening to me, do at least listen to me in these few hours that separate me from death. I have reserved them all for you alone. When you receive this letter I shall already be buried, and it may be that from that hour everyone will begin to forget me, until there will be no one who remembers my name. Listen to me therefore as a voice coming from the grave. You will mourn for my days which will have vanished like a dream in the night. You will lament our love which was useless and sad like the lamps which burn round the biers of the dead. Oh yes, Teresa, even my troubles had to have an end. And my hand does not shake as it takes hold of the liberating steel, since I am abandoning my life while you love me, while I am still worthy of you, and worthy of your tears, and I am able to sacrifice myself to myself alone, and to your virtue. No, you will not then be at fault in loving me. And I expect your love – I ask for it by virtue of my misfortunes, of my love, and of my tremendous sacrifice. Oh, if one day you were to pass by without glancing on the earth covering this unhappy young man, how wretched

I would be! I would have left behind me everlasting forgetfulness even in your heart!

You believe that I am going. So am I leaving you to new struggles with yourself, and to continual desperation? And while you love me, and I love you, and I feel that I shall love you for ever, do I leave you in the hope that our passion will die out before our lives? No, only in death, only in death. I have been digging my grave for a long time, and I am used to looking at it day and night, and coolly taking the measure of it – and in these extremes Nature recoils and cries out; but I am losing you, and I shall die. Even you yourself fled from me. We wept in rivalry. And were you not aware from my awful tranquillity that I wished to bid my last farewell to you, and that I was asking for an eternal farewell?

If the Father of men were to call me to account, I would show him my hands unstained by blood, and my heart unstained by crime. I would say, 'I have not taken the bread away from orphans and widows. I have not persecuted the unfortunate. I have not betrayed anyone. I have not forsaken my friend. I have not troubled the happiness of lovers, or polluted innocence, or alienated brothers from each other, or bowed down to wealth. I have shared my bread with the poor; I have mingled my tears with the tears of the afflicted. I have always wept over the misery of mankind. If you had granted me a homeland, I would have spent all my intellect and my blood on its behalf, and even so, my weak voice has courageously shouted out the truth. Almost corrupted by the world, after experiencing all its vices – but no, its vices may have infected me for brief moments, but they never conquered me – I have sought virtue in solitude. I have loved! You yourself, Lord, have shown me what happiness is. You have beautified it with the rays of your infinite light. You have given me a heart capable of feeling it and loving it. But after so much hope I have lost it all! And, useless to others and harmful to myself, I have freed myself from the certainty of perpetual misery. Do you enjoy, Father, the groans of mankind? Do you expect them to endure miseries which are beyond their strength? Or is it that you have granted mortals the power to cut their troubles short only so that they might neglect that gift of yours and drag on idly in the midst of weeping and guilt? And I do feel from my own experience that in extreme unhappiness nothing remains but guilt and death.'

Be comforted, Teresa. That God to whom you so piously have recourse, if he considers the life and death of a humble creature worthy of any care at all, will not withdraw his countenance even from me. He knows that I cannot hold out any longer. And he has seen the struggles I have had before reaching my fatal decision. And he has heard how often I have beseeched him to let this bitter chalice pass from me. Farewell therefore, farewell to the universe! O my friend, is the source of my tears still not exhausted? Once more I weep and tremble, but only for a short while. Soon everything will be annihilated. But my passions are alive and blazing, and they still possess me. Only when eternal night snatches the world away from me will my desires and my woes be buried with me. But my tearful eyes look for you before they close for ever. I shall see you, I shall see you for the last time, bid you my final farewell, and accept from you your tears, the only fruit of so much love!

I arrived from Venice at five o'clock, and I met him just outside his door as he was setting out to say goodbye to Teresa. He was dismayed by my unexpected arrival, and even more by my plan to accompany him as far as Ancona. He thanked me kindly and tried every way he could think of to dissuade me, but when he saw me insistent he fell silent, and he asked me to go with him to the T*** home. He did not speak on the way. He walked slowly, and there was in his face a certain sad resolution. Oh, I should have realised that at that moment he was turning over his last thoughts in his mind! We entered through the garden gate, and he paused, raised his eyes to the sky, and after some time he looked at me and burst out, 'Do you too think that today the light is more beautiful than ever?'

As we drew near to Teresa's rooms I heard her voice saying, 'But his heart cannot change.' I do not know whether Jacopo, who was one or two paces behind me, heard these words. He did not say anything in response to them. We found her husband there, taking a turn about the room, and Teresa's father seated at the end of the room by a small table with his head in his hands. For a long while we all remained silent. Finally Jacopo said, 'By tomorrow morning I shall not be here any more.' He went to Teresa and kissed her hand, and I saw tears in her eyes. Jacopo, still holding her hand, asked her to send for Isabella. The cries and tears of that little girl were so sudden and inconsolable that not one of us could *refrain from tears. As soon as she heard that he was going away, she flung her arms round his neck, and she kept sobbing, 'O my Jacopo, why are you leaving me? O my Jacopo, come back soon.' Not being able to resist such devotion, he put Isabella in Teresa's arms without saying a word. 'Farewell,' he said to her, 'farewell.' And he went out. Signor T*** went with him to the door of the house, and embraced him many times and groaned as he kissed him. Odoardo, who was by his side, shook his hand and wished him bon voyage.*

Night had already fallen, and as soon as we were at his house he told Michele to get the strongbox ready, and asked me to return immediately to Padua to pick up the letters which Professor C*** had shown him. And I went away forthwith. Then, under the letter which he had written to me that morning, he added this postscript:

Since I have not been able to spare you the sorrow of performing some final services for me – and I had already decided, before you came, to write to the parish priest about them – please add this last act of kindness to so many others. Have me buried, just as I am found, in a deserted place, at night, without funeral rites, without a stone, under the pines of the hill by the church. Bury Teresa's portrait with my body.

25 March, 1799.

Your friend, Jacopo Ortis.

He went out again. At eleven o'clock, finding himself at the foot of a hill two miles from home, he knocked at a peasant's door, and wakened him to ask for some water, of which he drank a great deal.

Coming home after midnight, he came quickly out of his room and gave the servant a sealed letter for me, telling him to give it to no one but me. Shaking his hand, he said, 'Farewell, Michele! Love me.' He gazed at him affectionately, then suddenly he left him, went back in, and closed the door behind himself. He continued the letter to Teresa.

ONE O'CLOCK

I have been to see my mountains, I have been to see Five Springs Lake, and I have said goodbye for ever to the woods, the fields, the sky. O my solitudes! O stream which first directed me to the home of that divine maiden! How often have I scattered flowers on your waters which flowed beneath her windows! How often have I strolled with Teresa along your banks, intoxicated with the pleasure of adoring her, and at the same time drinking great draughts from the chalice of death.

Sacred mulberry! I adored you too. I left you too with my last groans and my last thanks. I threw myself down, O my Teresa, beneath that trunk. And that grass has just drunk the sweetest tears which I have ever shed. It seemed to me to be still warm from the print of your heavenly body. It still seemed to me to be sweet-scented. That blessed evening is imprinted on my mind. I was seated at your side, Teresa, and the moon's rays shone through the branches and lit up your angelic face. I saw a tear run down your cheek. I drank that tear, and our lips and our breaths mingled, and my soul was transfused into your breast. It was the evening of 13th May, a Thursday. Since then not a moment has passed without my being comforted by the memory of that evening. I have considered my person as sacred, and have not deigned to glance at any lady, thinking them all undeserving of me – of me who has experienced all the blessedness of a kiss from you.

Well then, I loved you, I loved you, and I love you still with a love that cannot be understood by anyone but me. Death is a small price to pay, my angel, for one who has heard that you love him, and who has felt throughout his soul the pleasure of being kissed by you and weeping with you. I have one foot in the grave, yet even at this juncture you appear, as you always do, before these eyes which as I die are fixed on you, on you resplendent in all your sacred beauty. And it will be soon. Everything is ready. The night is already far advanced. Farewell. In a little while we shall be divided by nothingness, or by incomprehensible eternity. In nothingness? Yes, yes. Since I shall be without you, I pray God that, if he does not reserve for us a place where I may be reunited with you for ever, I pray from the depths of my soul, and in this awful hour of death, that he will abandon me in the void. But I die unstained, and in control of myself, and filled with you, and assured of your tears! Pardon me, Teresa, if ever – oh, be comforted and live for the happiness of our wretched parents. Your death would cause my ashes to be cursed.

If anyone should dare to blame you for my unhappy destiny,

confound him with this my solemn oath which I swear as I throw myself into the night of death: Teresa is innocent. Now receive my soul.

Michele, who was sleeping in the room next to Jacopo's apartment, was roused by the sound of a long-drawn-out groan. He pricked up his ears in case he was being called. He opened the window, thinking that I might have been shouting at the entrance, since he had been warned that I would return towards daybreak. But having assured himself that all was quiet and the night still dark, he went back to bed and slept. He told me later that the groan had frightened him, but that he had not paid too much attention to it, because his master was sometimes restless in his sleep.

In the morning Michele, having shouted and knocked on the door for a while, removed the bolt, and getting no reply from the first room, went forward uncertainly. And in the light of the lamp which was still burning, he saw Jacopo dying in a pool of his own blood. He flung the windows open, calling for someone to help, and since no one came running, he hurried to the doctor's house, but did not find him there because he was at the bed of a dying man. He ran for the parish priest, and he too was out for the same reason. He ran panting into the garden of the T*** home just as Teresa was coming out of it with her husband who was just telling her that he had got to know for certain that Jacopo had not gone away that night. She was hoping to say goodbye to him once more and, catching sight of the servant in the distance, she turned her face towards the gate through which Jacopo always came. With one hand she drew aside the veil which was falling over her forehead, and gazed intently, distressed and impatient to know for certain that he was coming. Then suddenly Michele was there, asking for help because his master had been hurt, and saying that he did not think he was quite dead. She listened to him without moving, with her eyes fixed all the time on the gate. Then, without a word or a tear, she fainted in Odoardo's arms.

Signor T*** rushed away, hoping to save his unhappy friend's life. He found him stretched out on a sofa with his face almost entirely hidden by cushions. He was motionless except that from time to time he panted. He had plunged a dagger beneath his left breast, but it had dropped out of the wound onto the floor. His black jacket and cravat were thrown over a nearby chair. He was dressed in waistcoat, trousers and boots. Round his waist was a broad band of silk, one end of which was hanging down bathed in blood. It may be that in his dying throes he had tried to unwind it from his body. Signor T*** gently lifted off his shirt, which was completely drenched in blood that had clotted on the wound. Jacopo came to, raised his face to him, and, looking at him with eyes growing dim in death, stretched out one arm as if to stop him, and with the other tried to clasp his hand. But he fell back again, with his head on the cushions, lifted his eyes to heaven, and breathed his last.

The wound was very long and deep, and although it had missed the heart, he had hastened his death by allowing the blood to flow: it was running in streams through the room. From his neck hung Teresa's portrait. It was quite black with blood, except where it was rubbed somewhat cleaner in the middle. And from Jacopo's bloodstained lips one can guess that in the throes of death he had kissed the likeness of his friend. On the writing-desk was the Bible, closed, and on that his watch. Nearby were various sheets of paper, on one of which was written: My dear mother. And from a few cancelled lines one could just make out the word: expiation. Then, lower down: of eternal weeping. On a further sheet only his mother's address could be read, as if he had regretted the first letter and begun another which he had not had the heart to continue.

As soon as I arrived from Padua, where I had had to stay longer than I wanted to, I was overwhelmed by the crush of peasants crowding silently under the porticos in the courtyard. Some of them looked at me dumbfounded, and one of them begged me not to go up. In fear and trembling I leapt into the room, and I was met by the sight of Teresa's father lying in despair upon the corpse, and of Michele on his knees with his face to the ground. I don't know how I had the strength to approach and place a hand on his heart near the wound. He was dead, and stone-cold. No tears or voice came, and I remained looking stupidly at the blood until the priest arrived, and immediately after him the doctor. Together with some of the servants they pulled us away from the grim spectacle. Teresa lived through all those days in a deathly silence amidst the mourning of her dear ones.

That night I trudged along behind his corpse which three labourers buried on the hill of pines.

1. An exact translation of a line from Gray's *Elegy*: *Even from the tomb the voice of nature cries.*

2. Dante, *Paradiso* xv. 118–20, slightly modified by Foscolo to suit his context.

3. Vittorio Alfieri, from a sonnet (*O cameretta, che già in te chiudesti*) about Petrarch's house in Arquà.

4. The first lines of three poems by Petrarch, respectively numbers 126, 129, and 192 of his *Canzoniere*.

5. Foscolo's own note says: 'This is a verse from the Bible; but I have not been able to find exactly where it occurs.' It looks like a vague reminiscence of the book of *Job*.

6. Dante, *Inferno* i. 87.

7. Petrarch, *Canzoniere*, poem 320.

8. Petrarch, *Canzoniere*, poem 18.

9. Napoleon, born in Corsica.

10. Dante, *Inferno* v. 102.

11. Dante, *Paradiso* xvii. 58–9.

12. Sterne, *A Sentimental Journey Through France and Italy*.

13. There are several echoes of Gray's *Elegy* in this paragraph.

14. Reference to the first edition of the book.

15. Alfieri.

16. *Exodus* xx. 5.

17. See *Of Tombs* 65–9.

18. Dante, *Inferno* vi. 4.

19. Alfieri, *Saul* ii. 2. Jacopo expects his reader to be aware of the context, especially the line: *All things are tears, and storm, and blood, and death.*

20. Dante died and was buried in Ravenna.

21. The Ionian Islands, ceded to France by the Treaty of Campoformio.

22. Alfieri, *Saul* iii. 4.

23. Alfieri, *Sofonisba* iv. 4.

24. *Trionfo della Morte* ii. 189–90.

25. *And legalised crime*: *De Bello Civili* i. 2. Lucan is, in his exordium, listing the themes of his poem.

26. Dante, *Purgatorio* i. 71.

Of Tombs

AN ODE FOR IPPOLITO PINDEMONTE[1]

Deorum manium iura sancta sunto.

XII TAB.[2]

Shaded by cypresses, and kept in urns
Consoled by weeping, is the sleep of death
Really not quite so rigid? When the sun
For me at length no longer fills the earth
With such a family of plants and beasts,
And when the hours to come no longer dance
Bright and illusory before my eyes,
And when, dear friend, I hear your verse no longer
With that sad music which decides its rhythm,
And when the spirit in my heart no longer
Speaks of the virgin Muses and of Love
(That spirit all that guides my wandering ways)
What solace for days lost would be a stone
Made to distinguish mine from other, countless
Bones which Death scatters over land and sea?
For truly, Pindemonte, even Hope,
Last of the gods to go, deserts the tomb;
Oblivion draws all things into its night;
A force that never tires wears all things out,
Never at rest; and man and tombs of men,
The final shape of things, and the remains
Of land and sea are all transformed by time.

But why – before time does – must man begrudge
Himself the illusion which, when he is dead,
Yet stops him at the doorway into Dis?
Buried, does he not go on living, with
Day's harmony to him inaudible,
If he rouse this illusion with sweet cares
In friendly memories? It is heaven-sent,
This correspondence of such deep affection,
A heavenly gift for human beings; and often
This means we go on living with our friend,
And he with us, if reverently the earth,
Which took him as a child and nourished him,
Offers a final refuge in her lap,
And keeps the sacredness of his remains

From outrage of the storm-clouds and profane
Feet trampling, and a stone preserves his name,
And fragrantly in bloom a friendly tree
Comforts his ashes in its gentle shade.

   Only who leaves no legacy of love
Has little joy in urns; and should he look
Beyond the funeral rites, he sees his spirit
Straying lamenting in the infernal regions
Or sheltering underneath the enormous wings
Of God's forgiveness: but he leaves his dust
To nettles spreading on untended turf,
Where neither loving woman offers prayers,
Nor solitary traveller hears the sigh
Which Nature sends to us out of the tomb.

   And yet today's new law sets tombs apart
From reverent glances, and denies the dead
Their glorious name. So now, Thalia, your priest[3]
Is lying untombed who, singing in your praise
Under his poor roof, cultivated laurel
With constant love, and hung up crowns to you;
Your laugh adorned those songs of his which hit
The Sardanapalus of Lombardy
Whose only pleasure lies in lowing herds
From Adda's hollows and the broad Ticino
Blessing his idleness with food and drink.
Where are you, Muse? I do not catch the scent
Ambrosia breathes, the token of your presence,
Among these shades where I sit down to sigh
My mother's house. And yet you used to come
And smile at him beneath that very lime
Whose drooping foliage shakes and shudders since
It does not shroud the urn of that old man
To whom it always lent such peace and shade.
Perhaps you stray among the meanest graves,
Searching to find where sleeps the sacred head
Of your Parini? Not a tree to shade him

Inside that city's walls, that city[4] lewd
Enough to harbour enervated singers!
No stone, no word! His bones may well be bloodied
By contact with the severed head of one
Who left his crimes but only on the scaffold.
You hear her scraping over thorns and rubble,
That sad abandoned bitch that roams around
Among the grave-pits, howling out of hunger;
You hear the hoopoe flutter from the skull
In which she shunned the moon, and flit through crosses
Scattered about the sombre countryside;
You hear that unclean bird reproach with mournful
Sobbing those rays the pitying starlight sheds
Upon forgotten graves. In vain, O Goddess,
You pray for dew to fall upon your poet
Out of the dreary night. Above the dead
No flower arises if it be not honoured
With human praises and with love's lament.

　　When that day came when marriage, laws, and altars
Gave to the human animal respect
Both for himself and others, then the living
From bitter weather and wild beasts abstracted
Those pitiful remains which Nature destines
To everlasting change and further ends.
Then tombs were witnesses to deeds of glory,
Altars for those who follow; from them came
The household gods' responses; oaths were awesome,
Oaths sworn upon the dust of ancestors:
This was the cult which, though the rites might vary,
The love of fatherland and family
Transmitted through the long succeeding years.
Not always have sepulchral stones been used
To pave our temples; nor involved in smoke
Of incense has the stench of corpses blighted
Those praying; nor have towns been always sad
With pictured skeletons (I see the mothers

Bound from their beds in terror, and extend
Their naked arms above the precious brows
Of their dear babies lest they be disturbed
By the protracted groaning of the dead
Who beg their heirs to buy a prayer for them
Out of the sanctuary); but cypresses
And cedars, loading zephyrs with their scent,
Stretched everlasting green above the urns
In everlasting memory, and precious
Vases were there to take the votive tears.
Friends used to snatch a sparkle from the sun
To illuminate the subterranean dark,
Because the eyes of dying men search out
The sun, and every breast exhales at last
One final sigh towards the light that flies.
Springs, always pouring out their lustral waters,
Fostered the amaranth and violet
On the funereal turf; and he who sat there,
To offer bowls of milk and tell his grief
To the departed, sensed a fragrance round,
As though a breeze that breathed Elysium.
A fond illusion! Which endears suburban
Gardens of tombs to girls who grieve in Britain;
They, guided to those gardens by the love
Of their dead mothers, linger to beg mercy
From Spirits of homecoming for the hero[5]
Who had the captured ship truncated by
Its tallest mast, and hollowed thence his coffin.
But where the rage for fame lies sound asleep,
Where opulence and dread are ministers
To civic living, then mere useless pomp,
Or worse, ill-omened images of Orcus,
Are monumental pillars made from marble.
The learned already and the rich and noble –
The mind and ornament of Italy –
Are tombed alive in sycophantic courts,

Armorial bearings all their praise. For us
May death prepare a place where we may rest,
Where fortune in the course of time must cease
From persecution; and may friendship gather
No heritage of hoarded wealth, but warmth
Of sentiment and independent song.

    The urns of strong men stimulate strong minds
To deeds of great distinction; and these urns
Make sacred for the traveller that earth
Which holds them. When I saw the monument
Where lies the body of that famous man[6]
Who, teaching rulers how to wield the sceptre,
Stripped laurel from it, and revealed to all
What tears it drips with and what drops of blood;
And saw the tomb of him[7] who raised in Rome
A new Olympus; and the tomb of him[8]
Who saw new worlds spin through the vaulted ether
Enlightened by the sun that shines unmoved,
And, for the Englishman[9] to spread his wings,
First cleared the pathways of the firmament –
Then I cried: Bless you Florence for your gentle
Breezes so full of life, and for your waters
Running from ridges of the Appennines!
Happy in such an atmosphere the moon
Clothes with her clearest light your clustered hills
Where grapes are gathering; and from your valleys,
Crowded with houses and with olive groves,
The incense of a thousand flowers goes up.
You were the first to hear the song that eased
The anger of the exiled Ghibelline;[10]
And you gave parents and an idiom
To him[11] through whom Calliope was vocal,
Who clothing Love in veils of purest white –
Naked in Greece, naked in ancient Rome –
Restored Love to the lap of heaven's Venus.
Blessèd because one temple[12] still preserves

Italy's glories, and her only glories
Now that the ill-defended Alps and all
The variability of human fate
Have spoiled her of her arms and wealth and altars
And nationhood, and left but memory.
When hope of glory comes to shine at last
On ardent intellects of Italy,
We shall draw portents hence. And to these marbles
Vittorio[13] often came for inspiration.
Angry with his own land, he wandered silent
Where Arno is deserted, looking longing
At fields and sky; and when he found no sight
Or living thing to mitigate his grief,
That stern man halted here, upon his face
Death-pallor manifest and also hope.
With these great men for ever, he inspires
Love of his native land. Oh, out of that
Religious peace there is a Spirit speaking:
It nursed against the Medes at Marathon,
Where Athens dedicated tombs to heroes,
Greek valour and Greek ire. The mariner
Sailing that sea which lies beneath Euboea
Observed beyond the spacious dark the lightning
Of flashing helmets and of clashing swords,
The pyres of blazing smoke, and saw the shapes
Of spectral warriors in burnished arms
Seek out the battle; heard grim silence shattered
By uproar of the phalanxes extending
Into the plains by night, a sound of trumpets,
A constant press of horses rushing up
To trample on the helmets of the dying,
Lament, and triumph, and the singing Fates.

　　How fortunate, Ippolito, when young,
To roam the spacious sea, the realm of winds!
And if the helmsman ever steered your ship
Beyond the Aegean Isles, you must have heard

The shores that line the Hellespont resound
With ancient deeds, heard the tide roar which washed
Achilles' arms up on the Trojan beach
Above the bones of Ajax. Death is just
In giving glory to the noble-hearted:
Not all his wiliness, no prince's favours,
Could keep Ulysses master of those spoils
Won with such effort; waves the gods below
Aroused removed them from his wandering ship.

I whom the times and appetite for honour
Compel to wander Europe as an exile,
I pray the Muses help me call up heroes,
The Muses who enliven mortal thought.
They sit as guardians of tombs; and when
Time with his chilly wings has swept away
The ruins even, then the Muses make
The deserts glad with song, and overcome
The silence of a thousand centuries.
Even today one place in barren Troas
Is still a wonder to the traveller,
Eternised by the Nymph who lay with Jove
And gave to Jove a son – that Dardanus
From whom came Troy, Assaracus, the fifty
Sons of great Priam, and the Julian line.
For when the nymph Electra heard the Fates
Calling her from the vital air of day
To the Elysian choirs, she breathed to Jove
This final prayer: And if, she said, you ever
Cherished my tresses, and my face, those nights
We lay awake in love, and if harsh fate
Withholds from me the best reward of all,
At least protect your dead friend out of heaven
That fame of your Electra may survive.
And with that prayer she died. The Olympian
Was moved and, bowing his immortal head,
He rained ambrosia down upon the Nymph

And made her body sacred and her tomb.
There Erichthonius lay, and there the ashes
Of Ilus rested; there the Trojan women
Would loose their hair, in vain alas, to pray for
Their husbands to avoid the impending fate;
Cassandra when the Deity within her
Forced her to prophesy Troy's mortal day,
Came there, and sang the shades a loving song,
And brought them their descendants, and instructed
The young men in the threnody of love.
She said with sighs: If ever out of Argos,
Where you will act as herdsmen for the horses
Of hard Ulysses, pitying heavens permit
That you return here, you will look in vain
To find your native land! The very walls,
The work of Phoebus, will be smoking rubble.
But gods, the Gods of Troy, will have a home
Within these tombs; it is a gift gods have,
To keep their proud name in the worst of plights.
And you, you palms and cypresses – whom Priam's
Daughters-in-law have planted, who will grow,
Too soon alas, watered by widows' tears –
Protect my ancestors! He who abstains
His axe from your devoted leaves will have
The less to mourn for from his flesh and blood,
And he will touch the altar with pure hands.
Protect my ancestors. The day will come
When you will see an old blind beggar[14] wander
Under your ancient shades, and feel his way
Into the burial place, and clasp the urns
And question them. Then all the hidden caves
Will murmur, and the mausoleum will tell
Of Ilium twice razed and twice arisen
In splendour high above the silent roadways
So that the final triumph might be greater
Won by the fateful Greeks. The sacred poet,

Soothing those troubled spirits with his song,
Will make the Argive kings immortal over
All lands embraced by the great father, ocean.
And you, Hector, will have your meed of mourning
Wherever men hold holy and lament
The blood shed for the homeland, while the sun
Continues shining over human grief.

NOTES

1. Foscolo wrote this poem in 1806, after some discussion of burial customs with the poet Ippolito Pindemonte (1753–1828), and as a response to the current application to Italy of Napoleon's Edict of Saint Cloud, which imposed burial outside inhabited areas, and plainness and uniformity of graves, on all classes of people.

2. *The rights of the sacred shades must be inviolable. (The Twelve Tables).* The Twelve Tables were a code of Roman law published 451–450 BC.

3. The poet Giuseppe Parini (d. 1799).

4. Milan.

5. Nelson.

6. Machiavelli.

7. Michelangelo.

8. Galileo.

9. Newton.

10. Dante.

11. Petrarch.

12. The Basilica of Santa Croce, in Florence.

13. The poet and dramatist Vittorio Alfieri (d. 1803).

14. Homer.

Niccolò Foscolo was born in Zante in 1778, the son of Andrea Foscolo, an impoverished nobleman, and Diamantina Spathis, a Greek peasant. He spent his early years in Split (Dalmatia) where his father worked as a physician. Following the death of his father in 1788, he moved first to Zante, and then joined his mother in Venice in 1792. Once in Venice, he became heavily involved in the city's literary circles and quickly gained a reputation as a writer and poet. (It was in 1795 that he chose to change his name to Ugo.) In 1797 he found fame for his tragedy, *Tieste*, a work that is noted for its controversial anti-tyrannical theme.

Devoted to Venice, Foscolo passionately believed that the city's greatest hope lay with Napoleon, and so fought under him against the Austrians. Venice was, however, ceded to Austria in 1797 with the Treaty of Campoformio. Unable to settle in the now Austrian-governed Venice, he spent the next years travelling, and fighting, throughout Italy and France, before moving to Switzerland. He finally exiled himself to London in 1816, where he first enjoyed considerable social success, but then soon fell into poverty and despair.

These feelings of disillusionment and betrayal pervade much of his writings, and in particular are found in his epistolary novel, *Last Letters of Jacopo Ortis*. Best remembered as a poet, he found his greatest powers of expression in his sonnets and in his masterpiece, *Of Tombs*, written in 1806. He died, still in exile, in 1827, and his grave remains in Chiswick old cemetery to this day.

J.G. Nichols is a published poet and translator. Amongst others, he has translated the poems of Guido Gozzano (for which he was awarded the John Florio Prize), Gabriele d'Annunzio, Giacomo Leopardi and Franceso Petrarch (for which he won the Monselice Prize).

SELECTED TITLES FROM HESPERUS PRESS

Gustave Flaubert *Memoirs of a Madman*
Alexander Pope *Scriblerus*
Anton Chekhov *The Story of a Nobody*
Joseph von Eichendorff *Life of a Good-for-nothing*
Mark Twain *The Diary of Adam and Eve*
Giovanni Boccaccio *Life of Dante*
Victor Hugo *The Last Day of a Condemned Man*
Joseph Conrad *Heart of Darkness*
Edgar Allan Poe *Eureka*
Emile Zola *For a Night of Love*
Daniel Defoe *The King of Pirates*
Giacomo Leopardi *Thoughts*
Nikolai Gogol *The Squabble*
Franz Kafka *Metamorphosis*
Herman Melville *The Enchanted Isles*
Leonardo da Vinci *Prophecies*
Charles Baudelaire *On Wine and Hashish*
William Makepeace Thackeray *Rebecca and Rowena*
Wilkie Collins *Who Killed Zebedee?*
Théophile Gautier *The Jinx*
Charles Dickens *The Haunted House*
Luigi Pirandello *Loveless Love*
Fyodor Dostoevsky *Poor People*
E.T.A. Hoffmann *Mademoiselle de Scudéri*
Francesco Petrarch *My Secret Book*
D.H. Lawrence *The Fox*
Percy Bysshe Shelley *Zastrozzi*